THE SMOKING GUN

The school field was still damp with dew as the Dearings security officer marched to the patch of land monitored by video camera E5. He expected to find a sad, bewildered old man with a straggling white beard, wearing a greasy raincoat and clutching a dubious bottle of alcohol. He wasn't prepared for the cold, lifeless body of a smartly dressed young man . . .

POINT CRIME

THE SMOKING GUN

Malcolm Rose

■SCHOLASTIC

Scholastic Children's Books,
Scholastic Publications Ltd,
7–9 Pratt Street, London NW1 0AE, UK

Scholastic Inc.,
730 Broadway, New York, NY 10003, USA

Scholastic Canada Ltd,
123 Newkirk Road, Richmond Hill,
Ontario, Canada L4C 3G5

Ashton Scholastic Pty Ltd,
P O Box 579, Gosford, New South Wales,
Australia

Ashton Scholastic Ltd,
Private Bag 1, Penrose, Auckland,
New Zealand

Published by Scholastic Children's Books 1993

Copyright © Malcolm Rose 1993

ISBN 0 590 55287 2

Typeset by Quadraset Ltd, Midsomer Norton, Avon
Printed by Cox & Wyman Ltd, Reading, Berks

10 9 8 7 6 5 4 3 2 1

For my grandmother

1

On your marks! The starter's pistol was raised aloft. One hundred metres down the track, two excited first-years held a ribbon across the lanes. In what the children called the Royal Box, the Head sat between his deputy, the unsmiling Mr Monk, and Dr Dearing, a representative of local business and Chairman of the School Governors. On the opposite side of the field stood the tall brick wall, topped by spikes and security cameras, that surrounded Dr Dearing's laboratories. Around the field, several elderly residents sat out on their porches, anticipating a good afternoon's competition.

Sports Day. David Rabin's mother and grandfather had turned up for the occasion. They had really come to see his sister, Ros, perform. She was the sporty one. David was not so athletic. He did have real strength – he had been forced to be strong since the death of his father – but it was strength of character in his case. There was another reason for the Rabin family's attendance at the school's annual event. As new residents in the area, they thought it appropriate to be seen for the first time at a school function.

Ever since their arrival in Northampton, Ros had been conscious of the wilder rumours circulating about them – the wealthy, fatherless newcomers. David himself was not aware of the gossip because he did not mix well at school. Perhaps it was because he was aloof that people gossiped. When Ros had convinced the rest of the family that they had become curiosities, David had decided that they should make this public appearance. He had not known then what an impact they would have on Sports Day.

Get set! The last shout of encouragement before the hubbub died away was Kevin's roar, "Come on, Ros – show 'em what you can do!"

In the third lane Ros arched on fingertips and toes, muscles tense. The silence invited a gunshot.

Suddenly, a noise broke the spell. Three of the sprinters set off, but pulled up when they realized that the starter's pistol had not fired. Not a shot, the noise was a cry. It sounded like the dreadful howl of a dog, mortally wounded. But it was emitted by a human. Someone in the crowd of spectators. Quizzical faces turned towards the massed ranks of parents.

In what used to be the caretaker's cottage, Mr Smith shuffled in his seat, curious to see what had happened. Further along the boundary of the school grounds, Mr Edriss exclaimed, "Good grief!" A half-smoked cigarette tumbled from his lips to the ground. When the shock of the noise passed, he smiled broadly. Delighted to witness a disruption of the event, he mumbled to himself, "Serve them right if something's gone wrong. Sports Day, indeed!"

Some inner instinct told David who had uttered the inhuman yell. It was not possible to recognize the baying as his grandfather's voice, but he knew all the same. From the senior pupils' benches, David dashed across the track. He had nearly reached his grandfather by the time his mother overcame her stupefied silence and began to scream, "Help! Help!" Ignoring her, David dropped to the ground where his grandfather had toppled from his chair. He nursed his grandfather's head in his lap as the old man gasped for air and clutched at his chest in agony.

"Grandfather! Grandfather!"

It was no good. He could not hear. His body was racked with pain. If David had not been holding him, he would have writhed on the ground like a worm sliced in two by the ruthless blade of a spade.

In less than a minute, the fit was over. The old man's body went limp. His eyes opened and, after a few seconds, he recognized David peering down at him in horror. He tried desperately to say something, but was too exhausted and breathless to make himself heard. Even so, there was a look of sheer determination in his drawn face. There was something he had to say to his beloved grandson. He gasped and tried again. "David . . ." he whispered, hardly able to move his blue lips.

"Yes?"

"I saw . . ." The voice became inaudible. Set in a cold white face, his eyes portrayed bloody-mindedness. Stubbornly, he refused to die before he had delivered his message. Again he struggled to speak. "David."

"Yes, I can hear you." David put his ear close to his grandfather's lips and listened intently.

His grandfather murmured his final words and gave a long sigh. David looked up and glanced around. He was surprised by the size of the audience that had collected about them.

Stunned, his mother stammered, "Has he gone?"

David said nothing. He just nodded.

His mother's hand darted to her mouth. She was too shaken even to weep. Through her fingers, she mumbled, "Oh, no! What did he say?"

David hesitated. "I . . . er . . ." He scanned the onlookers before he answered her. "I don't know, Mother. I couldn't make it out."

"What?" His mother was in shock and almost hysterical. "Did you see his face? Whatever he had to say was . . . so important to him. Are you sure you missed it?"

"Leave it, Mother. Now's not the time."

David continued to cradle his grandfather. He didn't need to check his pulse. He knew that the person he respected most in this world was dead. His death would be attributed to a heart attack, of course. But it wasn't that simple. David knew that the attack had been brought on by something his grandfather had seen, or thought he'd seen, on Sports Day.

He stroked the old man's white hair and closed his staring eyes. His grandfather had had a fraught life. Years of pain and bitterness had left their mark on him. But now that life had gone, his face expressed peacefulness. It bore the contentment of a man who had lived long enough to fulfil his ambition.

David was ashamed to cry before an audience. It betrayed a certain weakness that did not become the head of the family, and its only surviving male. But he could not help himself. His grandfather had meant so much to him. Now their relationship was over and the spent body lay before him like an exhausted runner who has successfully passed on the baton. David had not admitted it to his mother, but he *had* heard his grandfather's dying words. At least, he had heard enough of them to make sense. Now it was as though he held the baton securely in his grip and had no choice but to run with it. His grandfather's parting message seemed almost unbelievable, but he had struggled so much to deliver it that David had to take it seriously. A precious and gruesome heirloom had been handed down to him – a legacy that was too dangerous to share with his mother or with Ros. Even as he sat there, still holding the empty body of his grandfather, he knew that he would never benefit from this bequest.

And three weeks later, the sinister inheritance claimed its next victim.

2

It took Ros a few minutes to realize that the rocking sensation was not part of a dream, but that someone was trying to wake her. She opened her eyes and, in the dark, made out David's silhouette. "What. . . ?"

"Wake up."

Ros glanced at the bedside clock. "David! It's the middle of the night." She turned away from him.

"Yes. But we have to talk. Not for long."

Ros groaned. As usual, though, she gave up the notion of a good night's sleep and gave in to her brother. Keeping the sheet up to her shoulders, she heaved herself into a sitting position. "What is it?" she asked grumpily. "An apology for this morning at school?"

David perched on the edge of her bed. "What do you mean?"

"You really don't know, do you?" Ros replied in exasperation. "This morning. Your . . . outburst with Kevin."

"I'm not here to talk about that. This is something really important. Listen to me."

The remnants of sleep were pushed aside by Ros's anger. "Important! *My* life's important. You may be a tower of strength to Mother, but to me you're a pain. An arrogant . . ."

David interrupted her. "I was only thinking of you – protecting you . . ."

"I don't need protecting from Kev."

"You mean, you don't know that you need protection. There's a big difference."

Ros hated David in his Big Brother mode. He had taken exception to Kevin's interest in her and was determined to keep them apart. Kevin came from the wrong part of town. His family's income was inappropriate. And friendship with anyone having a criminal record was, to David, unthinkable. But Ros found him exciting, macho – and very good-looking. Her brother's attempt to break up their lunchtime liaison had ended in blows. Well, one blow. Kevin had delivered his direct and blunt response, a punch to the head, before David got to the end of a speech on how he failed to come up to scratch as a companion for Ros. Looking on,

Ros had found it difficult not to gloat as David picked himself off the floor.

"Kev's all right," Ros insisted. "You've never tried to get to know him. You deserved what you got, acting like a complete idiot."

David sighed. "As I said, I was only doing what's best for you," he replied paternally. "And what's best is . . ."

"Leave me to get on with my own life, David! I'm not your little sis, needing advice."

"I think you do. You'll see. Kevin is . . . not going anywhere. He needs sorting out."

"What do you mean?" Ros asked.

"I mean . . . Never mind. Look, I didn't come to talk about him. I came to tell you I'm going out."

"What?" Ros was so disarmed by her brother's sudden change of tack that she didn't insist on an answer to her question. "It's one o'clock!"

"I told you it was important."

"What are you going on about?"

"I'm sorry but I can't tell you. It's too . . . risky. Best if you keep out of it." Usually, David was very sure of himself. Now, he seemed insecure. "I came to give you this," he said to her.

For the first time, she noticed that his hands were not empty. He was carrying a torch and holding something out to her. She could not make it out in the dark.

"What is it?" she asked. "A postcard? I can't see."

David stood up. "Don't worry about it now. It's a photo."

"A photo?" She squinted at it.

"Yes. Of Grandmother. But don't bother about it now. If all goes well, I'll have it back in the morning." He hesitated then added, "It's a memento. You should keep it if anything goes wrong."

"Goes wrong?" Unnerved by his air of mystery, Ros asked, "What *is* all this, David?"

"I told you. It's too . . ." He edged his way towards the door.

"Yeah, yeah. Risky. Too risky for little sis. I suppose you're protecting me again," she said sarcastically.

"That's right," he replied from the doorway.

Suddenly, Ros remembered the incident with Kevin that morning. "You're not going to do anything silly, are you? To get your own back?"

David was too far away for Ros to see the expression on his face but his hesitation told her that she had stumbled upon something. His reply evaded her question. "I have to go now." The bedroom door clicked shut behind him.

"David!" she called. But it was no use. He had gone.

Ros turned on the bedside light and stared at the photograph in her hand. It was ancient, black and white, and tattered. It showed a woman in her twenties – her grandmother, if David was right

– standing against a whitewashed wall. She was shown in profile, wearing pyjamas. She looked unkempt and, if she hadn't been pregnant, she would have been unnaturally thin. Where it was visible, her skin was tight on prominent bones. Her hair, cropped short, hadn't seen a comb for some considerable time and her face was gaunt. The photo reflected hopelessness, sadness and resentment.

Shaking her head in perplexity, Ros put down the photo and slid out of bed. Pulling her bedroom curtain aside, just enough to peer round, she watched her brother's outline as he strode purposefully down the drive, carrying a plastic bag. She let go of the curtain when she could not make him out any longer. "What *is* going on?" she mumbled to herself. She knew that, despite the time of night, she must phone Kevin to warn him – just in case David was on his way with vengeance in mind.

3

"What's that, d'you reckon?" The two security guards at Dearing Scientific peered at the video screen. "It's . . . er . . . a shoe. Isn't it?"

"Mmm. Could be."

By the first light of day, the perimeter cameras normally picked out discarded crisp packets, empty Coke cans and dogs with their legs cocked against the wall. Items of clothing were a relative rarity.

The first security officer was still not satisfied. "The camera's panned as far as it'll go, hasn't it?"

"Yep," the other guard confirmed.

"Pity."

"Why?"

"Because I think there's a foot in the shoe."

"Yeah?"

"Yes. Look." He pointed at the extreme left of the screen where the black shoe was lying on a green background. "Isn't that a bit of sock?"

"I don't know. You might be right. Could have a drunk on our hands."

The other guard sighed. "Could be. You know what this means, don't you? Someone's got to go and check."

"Yeah, I know. I'll do the honours. You stay here and keep shop."

The school field was still damp with dew as the Dearings security officer marched to the patch of land monitored by video camera E5. He expected to find a sad, bewildered old man with a straggling white beard, wearing a greasy raincoat and clutching a dubious bottle of alcohol. He wasn't prepared for the cold, lifeless body of a smartly dressed young man.

Behind the screens that the police had erected in the playing fields, one man was taking photographs. Another was inspecting the body carefully with gloved hands. Detective Superintendent Whyte slipped into the tent and glanced at the victim, splayed on the grass. He groaned aloud.

His colleague, working on hands and knees, looked up. "Not very pleasant, Charlie. A lot of vomiting, evacuation of bowel and bladder."

Frowning, Detective Superintendent Whyte squatted down by the body. "So I see," he murmured. "Do we know who he is?"

"No. Nothing to identify him. He's still got his wallet, though – with money in it."

"Not a robbery, then. How about time of death?"

The pathologist shrugged. "I'll let you know."

"Best guess?"

"I'd say . . . between two and three. Yes. Four hours ago."

"Okay. Anything else yet?"

The pathologist lifted one of the boy's arms and pointed to red marks on his wrist.

"Been tied?"

"Yes. Both hands. At some point they were tied together. Probably behind his back. Maybe behind a chair. I need to examine the upper arms properly back in the lab to be sure."

"Tied with what?"

The pathologist shrugged. "More than string but not rope. Cord maybe."

"What about clothes?"

"Nothing very illuminating. Judging by the grass stains, he was writhing about here for some time."

Charlie Whyte mumbled, "Poor sod. How old do you think he is?"

"Seventeen? Eighteen at the outside."

"Not a nice age for this."

"No age is a nice age for this, Charlie," the pathologist replied.

"True, but the young ones are the worst. Anyway," the detective said, rising and stretching his legs, "what about the big question. Cause of death. Any answers?"

"Unknown at this stage," his colleague answered, looking up at him. "No obvious wounds. The only signs of violence so far are the marks on the wrists and a black eye."

"No one dies from a black eye or tied-up wrists. Any chance the black eye came from falling over here?"

"No. Not without breaking his nose as well. I imagine he's been thumped recently."

Charlie smiled wryly. "I thumped a few at that age. None of them died, though."

"Well, I've got a funny feeling about this one."

"In what way?"

"Cause of death," the pathologist answered. "It's a funny one."

"Great! That's all I need." Detective Superintendent Whyte headed for the gap in the awning. "Let me know. I'll be waiting. And don't make it too funny."

"There is one thing," the pathologist called after him.

Turning, Charlie prompted eagerly, "Yes?"

"By the smell, I'd say he was drunk."

"Drunk enough to kill him?"

"It's one possibility. It would explain the vomiting."

"Okay," the detective superintendent said. "Keep me informed." He left to talk to the press and await a telephone call from some anxious parent wanting to report a missing son.

In the field an army of uniformed policemen inched forward on hands and knees, radiating out from the canopy and peering closely at the ground for clues. They looked almost comical, like a pack of dogs trying to pick up an intriguing scent. Charlie wasn't laughing, though. He too had a funny feeling about this case.

4

And then there were two.

Ros clasped her frail mother in a vain attempt to console her. Mrs Rabin was rocking to and fro repeating over and over again, "Not David as well. What are we going to do now?"

After she had called the police to report his absence, she'd been put through to Detective Superintendent Whyte. He had rushed directly to the house. Even before he'd handed her the polaroid photograph of a boy to examine, she had known it was her David. Over the years she'd experienced so much misfortune that she had come to expect it. First, the exhaustion of caring for David's sick father and the tragedy of his death. Now, in rapid succession, both David's grandfather and David himself had died. This new blow was too much for her. She was drained.

Through her sobbing, she asked the policeman, "How did he . . . you know?"

Detective Superintendent Whyte spoke softly, with an air of business-like sympathy. "We don't know – yet. But we'll find out. Of course," he added, "I'll have to ask you to identify him."

David's mother took her handkerchief away from her tormented face. "But I already have! The photograph."

"I'm afraid you'll have to look at David himself. To make absolutely sure."

The policewoman who accompanied Detective Superintendent Whyte added, "It's made as easy as possible for you. It won't be as painful as you think."

Detective Superintendent Whyte nodded. "I have some questions for you as well." He glanced at Ros and added, "Both of you. I won't bother you too much now – I'll come back tomorrow. But, just to be getting on with, have you any idea what he was doing out in the middle of the night?"

Mrs Rabin shook her head. "He should have been here – safe," she sobbed.

"How about you? Rosalind, isn't it?"

"Yes. Ros." She hesitated, gulped and then said, "No. I've no idea what he was up to."

"Okay. What about fighting recently? Did he get into a fight?"

David's mother shrugged, speechless. Ros felt her cheeks reddening, but replied, "Er . . . I guess so. He had a black eye but . . . I don't know about it."

The detective rose. "Okay. Now's not really the time. Tracey here", he indicated the policewoman, "will hang on in case there's anything we can do. Or in case you want to talk about it. But just one more thing. Did David drink at all?" he asked.

"What? Alcohol, do you mean?"

"Yes."

"Certainly not," his mother replied, aghast.

Ros shook her head to confirm her mother's answer.

"Thanks," he said, keeping any views to himself. "I'm sorry about the questions but I have to . . ."

Mrs Rabin nodded, signifying that she understood.

"I'll come back later. Okay?" He looked at Ros and said pointedly, "Then maybe you'll be ready to tell me who gave him that black eye."

Ros's head dropped as she blushed again.

Ros phoned Kevin from her bedroom, well out of Tracey's hearing. When he came on the line, she said, "Kev? Is that you?"

Recognizing her voice, Kevin leapt in. "Hi, Ros. Have you heard? Someone's found a body – a dead body – on the school field. Wicked!"

Ros tried to respond but was lost for words.

"Ros?"

"Yes," she said. "I'm here. It's . . . It's David."

"What's David? What's up with him now?" Kevin sounded disdainful.

Ros felt awkward and foolish because the right words wouldn't come. She could only repeat, "It's David."

Kevin didn't reply immediately. It took a while for Ros's meaning to dawn on him. "David? In the field? You're kidding!"

"I'm not."

"Oh." Kevin paused again. "I don't know what to say, Ros. I'm sorry. It must be . . . rough."

"Rough? Mother's absolutely devastated."

"I guess so," Kevin replied. "Look, I'd better come over."

"No!" Ros suddenly became animated. "The police are here."

"So what?"

"They want to know where he was last night, and what he was doing. I thought he was going to your place to get his own back. Remember, I told you on the phone."

"Well, he didn't turn up here," Kevin assured her. Then, as he realized the full implication of what she had said, he added, "You mean, he was done in and they suspect me?"

"I don't know. They haven't found out yet. But they were asking about his black eye. If they discover it was you . . ."

"Damn!"

"Kev? Are you all right?"

"Yes," he answered. "I just . . . look, you believe me, don't you? We didn't get on, I know. We had a disagreement. But this is something else. I haven't seen him since school yesterday."

"Are you sure?"

"Ros!" He sounded indignant and defensive.

Ros wondered just how well she knew Kevin. She hadn't been seeing him for long and they had no friends in common. She hoped that her opinion of him wasn't as misguided as David had suggested. "Okay," she whispered. "I believe you." She tried to make her voice sound free of doubt.

She must have been successful because he replied, "I should think so."

"What should I do, though?" Ros asked him. "They'll quiz me about what I know. Tomorrow."

"Well, don't say he was coming here, whatever you do," Kevin said sharply. "You can't be sure he did anyway. But the punch-up's a different matter. You might as well tell them about that."

"Really?" she checked.

"If you don't, someone else will. They'll ask

around at school, no doubt. If it comes to a question of loyalty between me and Rabin – sorry, I mean, David – the kids'll back me. But there'll always be one who says too much. Someone'll let it out. They'll find out it was me all right, so you might as well come clean on that."

"Okay." Ros felt relieved to have his permission. She wasn't good at lying and dreaded trying to keep the truth from Detective Superintendent Whyte. "Of course," she added, "they'll be round to question you."

"Of course they will. I can handle it."

The more confident Kevin sounded, the more Ros's doubts about him returned. In his position, whether guilty or innocent, she would have been scared stiff by the thought of "helping the police with their inquiries". She didn't share Kevin's bravado in times of trouble. She hoped that their difference in attitude reflected nothing more sinister than a difference in upbringing.

"Ros?"

"Yes. Still here. Just . . . thinking."

"You sound pretty . . . shaken up. Not surprising, I suppose. I . . . er . . . I'm sorry, Ros."

Kevin had never seen eye-to-eye with David, and would never have done so. It was unlikely that he could summon up much remorse for David's death. It was quite likely, though, that he would feel genuine regret for Ros.

"What you need," he continued, "is a break. Get away from it for a while. How about the club tonight? I could pick you up. I just . . . came across a new motorbike. Bit clapped out but I've fixed it up okay . . ."

Ros interrupted his flow. "Kevin!" she exclaimed. "It's hardly suitable." She almost bit her tongue when she realized how like David she sounded. Still, it was true. "I can't . . . for lots of reasons. A disco's hardly the place for mourning. And, for another thing, I can't leave Mother."

"All right," he replied, apparently hurt. "I was just trying to help."

"Yeah. I'm sorry," she said as a peace-offering. "Guess we're all on edge."

She felt that Kevin's suggestion had been well meant, even if inappropriate. She could not believe that he didn't care, but realized that he must be finding it hard to pay his respects to someone for whom he had no respect. Ros wouldn't have admitted it to anyone, but she was having trouble coming to terms with her own feelings. She wasn't sure if her distress was caused by fear for the future rather than the tragedy of the present. Then there was anxiety for her mother. When she saw how her mother was suffering, Ros felt ashamed that she herself was not going through her fair share of grief. But, she told herself, someone has to keep a level head if the two remaining Rabins are going to

23

pull through. She had to assume the responsibility that had come so naturally to David. She was no longer the free-and-easy one in the family. She found herself wondering what she felt for David himself. She knew what she was supposed to feel, but she'd always had problems conforming to family expectations. In the school relay team, Ros had run the last leg. The ultimate responsibility for winning the race had been hers. Now, she felt like the last runner for the family as well. She understood that there would be new obligations, but she was unaware of the nature of another baton that David had surreptitiously passed on to her.

"For a while," she said to Kevin, "I've got to be here. Sorting things out. Mother's not capable of doing anything."

"Are you saying you're not seeing me again?" Kevin asked.

"No," she replied rapidly. "Just give me a bit of time."

"So when will we get together again?"

"I can't tell," Ros admitted.

"How about after the cops interview us? We should compare notes."

"Yes. Okay," Ros replied. "That makes sense. Give me a call and we'll take it from there."

"All right," Kevin concluded. "Knowing the cops, it won't be long. See you," he said. "And . . . all the best. You know."

"Thanks, Kev. Hope it goes all right with the police."

5

"What have you got for me, then?"

The pathologist laid down the woman's arm he was examining and turned to see Detective Superintendent Whyte. "Ah, Charlie," he said. "Just a moment." He gave some instructions to his deputy, peeled off his gloves and put them in the bin. "Over here," he called to the detective.

At a large sink, he talked while he scrubbed his hands. "Want to see the boy's body again, or just my report?"

"The report will do. But first, just tell me the main points."

"Okay. Prepare yourself," he began ominously. "Down the front of the lad's shirt was a stain." He indicated the place on his own white coat.

"The lab confirmed my suspicions. Residue of rum."

"Rum?"

Drying his hands on disposable towels, the pathologist said, "Yes. And enough alcohol in his urine to fail the test."

"So he drank himself to death?"

"No. There was something else on the shirt – and in the body."

"What?"

"I told you it was a funny one."

"You've got that wicked I-told-you-so look. Get on with it."

"It was a lethal dose of nicotine that killed him."

"Nicotine?" Charlie queried. "As in cigarettes?"

"That's right. Tobacco leaf extract."

"He smoked himself to death?"

"No. That takes years, not a few hours. Besides, it's not the nicotine that gets you when you smoke," the pathologist explained while they walked to his office. "Anyway, this lad didn't smoke. The presence of both rum and nicotine in the same stain on the shirt suggests they were taken together."

"You mean, someone prepared a lethal cocktail of nicotine in rum?"

The pathologist nodded. "Then forced him to drink it."

"Forced?" Detective Superintendent Whyte checked.

"Two things. Marks on the upper arms were consistent with his being held in a high-backed chair with his wrists tied behind it. And bruising around the mouth suggests forced entry – the bottle, presumably. The lad must have struggled a bit."

"So he was poisoned. Deliberately."

"You got it. Urine, blood and kidney – all riddled with nicotine." He took some notes from his desk and gave them to Detective Superintendent Whyte. "With the alcohol and loss of fluids, shock contributed to his death as well, but nicotine's the real villain of the piece."

The policeman glanced down the report as he asked, "Where do you get it from? And how much would you need?"

"It's all in there." The pathologist pointed to the papers. "The LD_{50} – that's the lethal dose, more or less – for someone his size would be about three grammes. But where do you get it?" He shrugged. "Any chemical suppliers, I guess. Nicotine used to be used as an insecticide, if I remember rightly, so it's not hard to come by – for someone who knows his chemistry." He hesitated, then added, "There's one other obvious place to get it from."

"Yes? Where's that?"

"A packet of ciggies, of course."

"Really? How? Is there enough nicotine in a packet?"

"I shouldn't think so. You'd need a good few packets, I suspect. I'm not a hundred per cent sure. You'll have to consult a tame chemist or toxicologist. But anyone who does a bit of chemistry would be able to extract it from tobacco."

"Wouldn't some special equipment be needed?"

"As I said," the pathologist went on, "better consult someone who knows. I'll tell you one thing, though. It's pretty neat as a murder weapon. Easy to get hold of. Ownership not illegal. And the forensic scientists can take as many samples as they like from suspects, it'll never prove anything. You'll get traces of nicotine just about anywhere and on almost everybody. Especially on – or near – smokers. Forget forensic evidence. It's like finding a drowned man in the middle of the Atlantic and asking exactly which bit of the water killed him."

"Okay," Charlie groaned, "I get the picture. Just tell me. Have you come across a poisoning like this before?"

"No," he answered. "It's definitely a funny one."

"Just my luck!" Charlie waved the report and said, "Anyway, thanks for this."

"You're welcome," the pathologist replied as he prepared himself to return to the examination of another victim. "If I were you, I'd drag out my old chemistry schoolbooks. A bit of revision is called for."

6

When Detective Superintendent Whyte returned to Ros's house, he was not alone. He was accompanied by Tracey, who had the impossible task of comforting Mrs Rabin, and another policeman, who was there to help sift through David's belongings. Such a search was needed, they explained tactfully, because their inquiries had become a murder investigation. David's effects might reveal a clue.

Mrs Rabin did not take the news well, and it was not long before Tracey called in the family doctor to put her under sedation. Then it was up to Ros to deal with Detective Superintendent Whyte and his questions on her own.

"If you believe in TV cops," he said to break the

ice, "you'd expect me to be called Super. But no one calls me Super. I can't think why not. Anyway, Charlie will do for me." He went on to ask her at length about her brother: his friends, his life, his state of mind, everything.

Eventually, he came to the topic that Ros had dreaded. "Now," he probed, "this black eye. You said you didn't know anything about it, but have you changed your mind?"

Head bowed, Ros simply nodded.

"Tell me about it."

"It was David's fault really," she began, from the outset defending Kevin. She knew she shouldn't speak ill of the dead, but it was the truth. Besides, there was nothing she could do for David now. At least she could protect the living. She explained how David had insulted Kevin by telling him that he wasn't good enough to mix with the Rabins.

Charlie Whyte made a note of Kevin's details then asked, "What did you think of this . . . spot of bother?"

"How do you mean?" Ros asked innocently.

"Did you approve of your brother's action?"

"No. David gets . . . He used to get too bossy. He meant well, of course. But he took his rôle as head of the family too seriously. We argued about it afterwards."

The policeman's ears pricked up. "Oh yes? When?"

Ros blushed. "It was . . . late. He came to . . . Anyway, we had a row about it."

"What time was this?"

"One o'clock."

"You sound sure. It's not a guess, is it?"

"No. I checked my bedside clock."

"And after you argued, he left? Left the house?"

Ros nodded again. "Yes. That's why he came into my room in the first place. To tell me he was going out."

"Strange at that time of night. It must have been important. Surely he said where he was going, or why he was going somewhere?"

"No." She dared not mention her suspicion that David had set out for Kevin's house. "He just came to say he was going out. That's all. He wouldn't tell me where when I asked him."

Detective Superintendent Whyte pondered for a moment. It was simple to deduce that Kevin might be involved. "Time, I think, that I had a word with Kevin Kingsnorth," he said.

"But he's not . . . It wasn't Kev that did it."

"No?"

"No. He's . . . not like that."

"I'm sure you're right, Ros," Charlie reassured her. "But I'd better check it out for myself. I have to."

"Yes. I know," Ros admitted sullenly.

"What did *you* do after David left?" Detective

Superintendent Whyte asked.

"Me?"

"Yes. You quarrelled about Kevin, then he left. What did you do?"

"You don't think I. . . ?"

"I just want to know what you did. Like, did you run after him?"

"No," she answered. "For one thing, I wasn't dressed. I'd never have caught him up by the time I'd got some clothes on." Until then, it hadn't crossed Ros's mind that she might be a suspect herself. She gulped at the thought. Suddenly, she didn't feel like answering any more questions. She wished there was someone there to advise her. Someone like David.

From that moment she decided to be less co-operative. She thought better of telling the detective about her phone call to Kevin. That would implicate him even more. He was in enough trouble without that. She also decided not to tell Detective Superintendent Whyte about the old photograph of Grandmother. It was something, she felt, that was private to the family, and telling the policeman about it would be a betrayal of some family secret that she didn't understand.

"I went to sleep. Nothing more," she said. "I took a while to settle, but that's all I did. Went to sleep feeling annoyed with him. Maybe even a bit worried about why he'd gone out. But it was the last time I saw him." She swallowed, trying not to show her weakness.

"It's okay, Ros," Charlie said warmly. "Look, I think I've bothered you enough for one night. I'll leave you in peace now. I'm sorry I've had to put you through this."

"I understand."

They both rose. On the way to the door, Detective Superintendent Whyte asked her, "How do you get on at school?"

"How do you mean?"

"Don't panic," he replied amiably. "Nothing to do with the inquiry. Just interested. What are your best subjects?"

Nonplussed, Ros said, "Er . . . I don't know. History, I guess."

"History! My worst," Charlie replied in a friendly tone. "Could never concentrate on the past. Always wanted to investigate the present myself. Science was my best subject. Chemistry. Are *you* interested in chemistry? Any good at it?"

Thinking that his banter was altogether out of place, Ros wanted to bring the conversation to an end as soon as possible. "No," she replied tersely. "Flopped Combined Science last year – at my old school."

"You're . . . what? First year of A levels?"

"Yes. History, English and Social Science."

"Well," Charlie said, opening the front door, "I

hope you can return to normal studies soon." He looked outside and up at the clouds. "Mmm. Looks like rain on the way." Glancing back at her, he added, "Thanks for your patience."

She nodded, then shut the door with a feeling of immense relief. After a few moments savouring privacy, she made for the phone. She had to warn Kevin that the police were probably on their way – and that they were hunting for a murderer.

7

Outside the long terrace of grey-brick houses, there were two cars without wheels, several abandoned shopping trolleys, a couple of Jehovah's Witnesses, and a stray dog. A man whose bare arms were covered in tattoos was wagging his finger at a young boy and shouting, "How many times have I told you. . . ?" Further down Curtis Street three boys were kicking a tin can across the road. Overhead, dark clouds drifted.

Detective Superintendent Whyte's car, driven by Tracey, meandered down the road to avoid first the footballers then the dog. It cruised past the tattooed man and his son, and pulled up outside number 37. The detective got out of the car and banged on the wooden door as if he were trying to waken the dead.

After a couple of minutes, Kevin answered the door. Neither of his callers were in uniform but he frowned and groaned. "Cops!" he muttered.

"Kevin Kingsnorth?" Detective Superintendent Whyte asked.

Before Kevin could reply, the black sky above them was rent by lightning, like a flashing blade slicing through a dark curtain. Almost immediately, ear-splitting thunder boomed and huge raindrops pelted down.

"Amazing!" Kevin cried above the clatter. "How did you do that?"

"Always like to make a dramatic entrance," the policeman yelled back.

"It'd be fun to keep you here on the doorstep," Kevin replied, "but I guess I'd better let you in." He stood to one side.

Already soaked, they stepped inside and dripped on to the living room carpet. "Thanks."

"What's it all about? David Rabin?"

Not responding straight away, the policeman introduced himself. "I'm Detective Superintendent Whyte and this is WPC Ashmore. And . . . er . . . Can I sit here?" He plonked himself down and tried to ease his wet trousers away from his skin. "I'd like to know why you think this is about David Rabin."

Kevin sat down opposite the policeman and smiled. "You must have asked around by now.

Found out who his friends were, and how many enemies he had. I imagine my name cropped up."

"Would you imagine it cropped up as a friend or enemy?"

"We . . . er . . . You wouldn't say we were the best of buddies."

"What would you say?"

"I'd say he was a pompous twit. More money than community spirit."

The policewoman remained on her feet, walking around the room and peering into every nook and cranny. Whenever she stopped circling, she kept her eyes on Kevin as he answered the questions.

"What was the problem between you, exactly?" WPC Ashmore asked.

Kevin smiled again. "Why keep beating about the bush when you want to know if I was the one who clobbered him?"

"Clobbered?" Detective Superintendent Whyte queried.

"Thumped," Kevin explained. "And yes, it was me. I thumped him. But the thump was the only thing I did to him."

"Only?"

"Yeah. Nothing else."

"Should there be anything else?"

"You wouldn't be here," Kevin retorted, "just to investigate a schoolyard tiff."

The rain clattered against the window like

handfuls of pebbles and the water sluicing the pane obliterated the view of the street. The next flash of lightning appeared at the window like the momentary glare of the headlights of a passing car. This time it took a few seconds before they were hit by a barrage of thunder.

"Police procedure is something you know all about, isn't it, Kevin? First-hand experience."

"Yeah, yeah. No need to go on about it."

"Arson, wasn't it?" the policewoman asked.

"You know exactly what it was," Kevin snapped. "You'd have checked up before coming."

"You see our problem, though," the detective superintendent said, leaning forward in his seat. "This is your second argument with some kid from the other side of town. The first gets a petrol-soaked rag and a match through the front door. The second . . . ends up dead in a field."

"I was younger, then. Besides, no one got hurt," Kevin protested. "And I didn't hurt anyone this time, either."

"Are your parents in?" the detective inquired.

"You've got to be joking! Out on the town as usual. They'll be back about two in the morning, if form is anything to go by."

The policeman leaned even further forwards and ordered, "Show me your hands."

"What?"

"Show me."

Detective Superintendent Whyte examined Kevin's fingers for yellow staining. "Mmm," he said, letting go the hands. "You smoke."

"I used to."

"Judging by the stains, you've given it up very recently. Why?"

"Can't afford it. And Ros objects as well. Why do you want to know?"

"Where did you buy them from, when you did smoke?"

"All over. The newsagent's round the corner usually. So what?"

"Never mind." The detective superintendent sat back in his chair again, then asked sternly, "Friday night. Between midnight and three a.m. Where were you?"

"Friday?" Kevin stalled.

"Yes. The early hours of Saturday, actually."

"I was here."

"Tucked up in bed?"

"No," Kevin replied. "Watching telly. Big match. Live."

"Match? What match?"

Kevin answered, "American Football. At San Francisco."

"Who won?" the policeman inquired.

"The home team. The 49ers."

"Did you watch it on your own?" asked WPC Ashmore.

"No. A couple of mates came round. Graham Johnson and Darren Cook."

"And they'll confirm this?"

"Yeah."

"And when they're next in trouble, you'll provide the alibi, eh?" Whyte grinned wryly but not unpleasantly.

Kevin shrugged. "I just told you the truth, that's all."

Detective Superintendent Whyte changed the subject again. "Tell me why you thumped him. Rabin, that is."

Kevin looked puzzled. "Won't you have heard this already, from Ros? She was there."

"You tell me."

"Prince Charming told me I was too low on the evolutionary scale to be mixing with his Ros."

"Anything else?"

"That was enough," Kevin replied wickedly. "He said some other stuff as well, but that was enough for me."

"How did Ros react?"

Kevin shrugged. "Ask her."

"But what do you think?"

"I think you ought to ask her if you want to know."

Whyte wouldn't let go. "Did she congratulate you?" he queried. "Or have a go at you for hitting her brother?"

"She didn't seem too upset to see Rabin get what was coming to him." It suddenly occurred to Kevin that the cops might even suspect Ros, so he said no more. He didn't want to get her into trouble by implying that she was purring quietly over her brother's death.

"Have you seen Ros since the fight?" Tracey put in.

"No. Well, only across a crowded playground at break on the same day." To take the heat off Ros, he added, "She's been too upset to see me since . . . you know."

Kevin was relieved that the accusing finger was not pointed only at him, but he was appalled that Ros was also under suspicion. Not Ros! She didn't get on with her brother, and she was now a lot closer to a fortune, but . . . surely not! Ros was too full of life to take it from anyone else. Then it struck him that they might even suspect a conspiracy between Ros and him. After all, they were a lot better off without Big Brother watching over them.

"What's your relationship with Ros Rabin?" the detective superintendent asked, as if to confirm Kevin's assessment of his predicament.

"It's . . . er . . ." Kevin shrugged. "We get along. Nothing too serious."

"But serious enough to annoy her brother."

"It didn't take much to do that," Kevin remarked.

The rain had ceased to batter the window. It had become a gentle patter and the thunder a distant rumble.

"How are you getting on at school?"

"School? Er . . . All right. Why?"

"You're the same age as Ros, right? But a year behind."

"That's the effect of my last run-in with you lot. It put me back a year at school."

"Do you know what LD fifty is?" queried Detective Superintendent Whyte.

"What's this? Some sort of test?" Kevin groused.

"Do you know?"

"Sounds like a grade of engine oil to me."

The policeman did not ask another question straight away. He examined Kevin's face and let the silence force the boy into saying more. "Well?" Kevin said in agitation. "Am I close? What is this LD fifty stuff?"

"I thought you'd know."

Kevin shuffled uncomfortably in his seat. "No. No idea. Some funny questions you're coming out with – even for a cop."

"Well, you know how he died, don't you?"

Kevin hesitated, then grimaced. "No," he answered. "You didn't say, and it's not been in the papers." He was relieved to be back on familiar territory. The famous elephant-trap of a police question. He could cope with that sort of trick question all day long. It was the questioning that he didn't understand that made him feel uneasy. "What did he die of?" asked Kevin.

"He was poisoned."

"Poisoned? Wow! What with?"

"Oh, I don't think we need to go into that," Detective Superintendent Whyte replied. "But we may take a look around your house – just in case there's traces of it here."

"Feel free," Kevin retorted. "Search as much as you like. We're clean."

"Okay, Kevin," the policeman said, rising to his feet. "We may do that. But not us. Some forensic chappies. Real experts. They don't miss a thing, you know."

Again, Kevin felt at ease with threats. He was used to intimidation. He would have been more anxious if the police had left without trying to panic him. "Fine," he replied in defiance.

"We'll be back," Detective Superintendent Whyte said as he went out through the door that the WPC had opened for him.

"Sure," Kevin called after him.

The storm had passed. It had gone to terrorize some other town. In the street outside number 37, rainwater had collected all around the parked car. As Tracey looked down at the puddles, she cried, "Oh, no!"

"What's up?" Charlie asked.

"Flat tyres. All of them. I'll have to call for back-up."

Charlie grinned at her and said, "As I've always told you, Tracey, know your environment. Know what you're getting into and take account of it."

"What?"

He walked to the back of the car and opened the boot. "The lads round here can recognize an unmarked police car by sixth sense. You should expect them to let the tyres down," he explained. He picked out a foot-pump and held it aloft triumphantly. "See? Forethought pays. I got the mechanics to put it in as soon as I decided to come here." He slammed shut the boot and said, "Come on. I'll do two tyres. You can do the other two. That's equality for you."

8

Ros was feeling vulnerable. She had always been sheltered from responsibility by the umbrella of the family. Now that umbrella had collapsed. If she didn't have the strength to hold it up, everything would collapse. Her mother hardly had the strength, or the will, to rise from her bed so it was Ros who had to take charge of the family affairs. Overnight, her freedom had been replaced with responsibility.

And on top of all that, there was Kevin. Was it right to be associating with someone suspected of her brother's murder? Should she be seeing him even before the police had released David's body for the funeral? Could she really be so certain of his good intentions? How on earth could she expect to run the family if she couldn't even make up her mind about Kevin?

After a little pressure from him on the phone, she'd agreed to see him. She wasn't sure whether belief in his innocence or curiosity about his encounter with the police had contributed more to her decision.

They met in the evening at Kevin's local youth centre, where a band of young hopefuls were playing cover versions fast, furiously and ineffectively. The singer cried to his colleagues, "Give 'em a belter. Let's have some life!" Even in a relatively quiet corner of the bar, Kevin and Ros couldn't make themselves heard without yelling at each other. "Come on," Kevin shouted. "I've got an idea."

They stood by the barricade to the swimming pool till no one was looking then, Kevin leading Ros by the arm, they vaulted over and into the changing rooms. "Here?" Ros queried.

"No," Kevin answered. "Let's go into the pool itself."

"What?" Ros objected. "You've got to be joking."

"No," Kevin explained. "I mean, sit by the pool."

"Oh. Okay."

They went through the shower area and sat at the edge of the pool on the seats reserved for the attendants.

"Mmm," Ros said. "This is quite nice. Calm."

Only a faint repetitive thump from the hall penetrated the walls. One side of the pool, entirely windows, let in the moonlight which reflected off the uncannily still water. If it hadn't been for the reflection and the characteristic smell of disinfectant, they would have thought the water had been drained away.

"I've never seen the water like this before," Kevin said quietly.

"It's like . . . asleep," Ros replied. "Eerie."

"Yeah."

For a while they sat in silence. Ros was enjoying the tranquillity and Kevin was wondering how to break the spell. He was keen to talk about the murder, but before he'd settled on an opening sentence that didn't seem heartless, Ros chipped in. "Well, we can't just sit here, I guess. We'd better get started."

Gratefully Kevin agreed. "Why don't I go first?"

Ros shrugged. "If you like. What did they ask you?"

"Oh, some standard stuff – and some funny things as well." He went through as much of the interview as he could remember, interrupting his flow now and again to make conclusions or to answer Ros's questions.

"Why did he ask about smoking?" asked Ros.

"Search me," he responded.

"Do you reckon they'll check up on what you said about watching telly?"

"Sure to. But Darren and Graham won't let me down. They'll swear they watched the game with me."

"So you didn't really? You don't actually have an alibi."

"No," Kevin admitted. "And you've got the same problem. Remember, you're on their hit list as well. Perhaps we should have said we were together. Thinking about it, though," he added, "they might suspect we're in it together, so that wouldn't have helped."

"No," Ros said. "Anyway, I can't lie without turning bright red."

"Oh," Kevin recalled suddenly, "they asked me what LD fifty is. I didn't know. Do you?"

"LD fifty?" Ros replied. "Yes. We did a project on animal experiments. It's the dose that's lethal for fifty per cent of a bunch of animals when they're fed some stuff that's being tested. They check out the LD_{50} of pesticides and things like that."

"So," Kevin queried, "it tells you how poisonous something is?"

"That's right," Ros confirmed.

"Ah, well. That makes sense, then. I passed that little test. They were trying to see if I knew how much of a poison to give someone to kill them. I didn't."

"You mean, David was poisoned?"

"Yes. Didn't you know?"

"They didn't tell me," she said. "I was in such a spin, I didn't think to ask."

"They wouldn't have said at first, anyway. They like to find out if a suspect knows the cause of death before it's publicized. Did this Whyte chap ask you anything about poisons, or something like it?"

"No," Ros replied. She hesitated then added, "Now you mention it, he did ask me something about chemistry. Whether I was any good at it. Was that my test? I guess it was. I hope I passed as well."

"Lucky he didn't give you the LD_{50} test. You'd have failed."

"No, he didn't ask me that one. Just as well, really."

"You'd better tell me what else they asked you," Kevin said.

To the barely audible heartbeat of the bustling life beyond the swimming pool walls, and hardly shifting her gaze from the becalmed water, Ros related her story. She also told him more of her encounter with David in her bedroom. "And," she finished gloomily, "a couple of hours later, he was dead."

Kevin squeezed her arm. "Yeah. I'm sorry."

"Are you?" Ros found herself saying. "Aren't you pleased to see the back of him?"

"That's not fair, Ros," Kevin replied, letting go of her arm. "He rubbed me up the wrong way, but . . ."

Ros looked at him askance, then wiped her eyes. "Okay," she said. "I trust you. I'm sorry. I'm still upset. I still expect him to come through a door – maybe walk in here and find us together. He'd throw a fit."

"Of course you're upset," Kevin said as sympathetically as he was able. "The way I see it, you and me have got to stick together, though. We've got the cops after us. So the sooner we work out who . . . did it, the sooner we'll be off the hook."

"Us?"

"Why not?" Kevin answered. "We know about as much as the cops. And you know a bit more. What was the photo he gave you?"

"Grandmother. When she was young – and pregnant. Do you think that's got anything to do with it? David didn't say it was important, not in so many words. He just called it a memento."

Kevin shrugged. "No idea if it's important. But we shouldn't rule it out. We'll have to look at it together. She's not . . . alive now, is she?"

"No," Ros answered. "She died soon after the photo was taken, I guess."

"This was the wife of the chap that died on Sports Day?" Kevin checked.

"Yes. Heart attack. Like Father when I was young."

"Your family's had it rough, hasn't it?"

Somewhere, a door opened then slammed shut. Ros didn't answer Kevin's question for a few moments. When the stillness returned and they were out of danger of being discovered, she whispered, "Yes. It's not a pretty history. But I don't know much about it. No one at home said anything. Not to me, anyway. David and Grandfather were close. They probably talked about it." Ross turned to Kevin and added, "The Rabin household could never have been described as a hotbed of feminism, you know. The men took care of the important things. Like a secret society, they were. I was left out in the cold – expected to help around the house and look decorative, that's all. They'd be regretting it now – keeping me in the dark – because I'll have to pick up the pieces."

"Well, what *do* you know?"

"I guess that photo must have been taken just before Grandmother had Father. She died giving birth." The quiet throb of the music relented for a few moments then started up once more, like a heart that stopped briefly, dangerously, before it began to pump life again. "It was a difficult birth all round, but I don't know the details. I bet David knew. Grandfather would have filled him in. They hid it from me. Made me feel . . . I don't know . . . bitter, particularly towards David. Perhaps that's why we weren't closer, because I felt isolated. Anyway, the birth left Father unhealthy for most of his life. Mother came along and helped him through – gave him a good few more years, I reckon. Strong in those days, she was. But looking after him sapped all her energy. By the time he died – his heart packed up, I think – she was a nervous wreck. I was five at the time."

"So how come he earned a fortune?" asked Kevin.

Ros shrugged. "That was Grandfather and Father between them. You don't need to be healthy to play the money markets – to buy the right currency and the right businesses at the right time. They were good at it. Green fingers for stocks and shares and all that."

"All this wheeler-dealing!" Kevin scorned. "But at the end of the day they haven't made anything useful – except money for themselves." He paused, then said, "Sorry, Ros, but I can't stand that sort of thing."

"I'm not keen myself," Ros answered. "But the point is, has any of it got anything to do with David?"

"I've no idea," Kevin replied.

"Nor me. I don't see how it could."

"What about David himself, then? Any clues there? Did you say he was carrying a plastic bag that night?"

"Yes. But I don't know what was in it — if anything."

"And he had a torch?"

"Yes. So?"

"So, did the police say they'd found a bag or torch?"

"No. Would they, even if they had?"

"They'd probably ask you to identify them. Was the torch special at all? Or did it have his name on it?"

"No. Not as far as I know," answered Ros. "It was . . . just ordinary. I dare say there are lots of them around."

"But would you recognize the type if you saw it again?" Kevin asked.

"Yes, I think so."

"Good. So that's three leads we've got that the law hasn't: the torch, the bag and the photo. The trouble is, they've got the murder weapon. They know which poison . . ." Kevin stopped talking because he could see that Ros was distressed by his enthusiasm.

"You talk about David as if he was just . . . I don't know," Ros muttered. "He hasn't even been buried yet and you're all excited about some detective caper."

"I'm sorry, Ros," he replied, lost for any other words.

"Besides," Ros added, "what if we did find out something?"

"What do you mean?"

"Wouldn't it be dangerous?"

Kevin looked puzzled. "How come?" he asked.

"David said it was risky. He wanted to leave me out of it. If we go chasing a murderer, wouldn't he protect himself? Maybe we'd be next in the firing line."

Kevin hesitated then replied, "No worries, Ros. We'll be careful."

Ros didn't know whether to be reassured or dismayed at his confidence. She sighed. "I've had enough," she said. "I'm going home."

"Okay," Kevin agreed. "Let's sneak out of here and I'll take you back on the bike."

They crept away from the dormant pool, passing through the turmoil of the disco and out into the cold dark night. "Want to risk a dodgy curry from the van?" Kevin asked, suddenly hungry.

"No," Ros replied quietly but firmly. "Just straight home."

9

Mr Monk, known amongst his pupils as Chip-monk because he seemed to have a chip on his shoulder, frowned at Detective Superintendent Whyte. "Yes. Rabin." He considered for a moment, wiping his perfectly bald head with his hand. "Not been here long and not one of my favourite pupils, I must confess. Bright, of course. Very bright. He'd have made it big, no doubt. Lucky lad."

"How do you mean," the policeman questioned, "lucky?"

"Some of us have to fight our way through life, Detective Superintendent," Mr Monk complained. "Even the able ones. Rabin was clever all right, but it wouldn't have mattered if he wasn't. The family business was always his safety net."

"Would you deny him his good luck, then?"

"When I was his age, we didn't have two pennies to rub together," the Deputy Head and science teacher replied. "It was hard to get even this far. Long hours, part-time jobs while studying – that sort of thing. Certainly no safety net. If I'd been free of those sorts of constraints, I'd have . . . Who knows? I wouldn't have got bogged down in a dead-end teaching job, that's for sure. I'd have been out there doing science, not teaching it. And earning a worthwhile salary."

Detective Superintendent Whyte nodded sympathetically, encouraging Chipmonk to show his true colours. "I know what you mean. There's lots like us. Hard work, little reward. Then there's the privileged classes . . ." He shook his head, signifying unspeakable injustice.

Recognizing that bait was being dangled in front of him, Chipmonk refused to bite. "Don't get me wrong, Mr Whyte. Rabin certainly was privileged, but I didn't resent it that much. Anyway," he added, "neither of us would want to be in his shoes now, eh? Even Rabin deserved better than what he got."

"True," Detective Superintendent Whyte agreed. "Anything else about him?"

"Not really," the teacher answered. "I just couldn't get on with him, that's all. Neither did his peers. Rather arrogant, I found."

"In what way?"

"Sure of himself. Let me give you an example. Earlier this year he chose to do a project on the environment for his science studies. Before we knew it, he was round at Dearings, asking to interview Dr Dearing himself. Wanted to know if Dearings had an environmental policy."

"When was this?" asked the detective.

"I don't know exactly – before his grandfather died at Sports Day. About five weeks ago, I'd say."

"Well, did he get to speak to anyone in authority?"

"I'm not sure. We only found out he was making a nuisance of himself because Dr Dearing phoned the school. No one minds inquisitiveness, of course. They gave him some literature on the labs and sent him away, apparently. After he'd read it, he was back with questions. They refused to give him any more information. He would hardly take no for an answer. Persistence bordering on provocation. Unacceptable in any circumstances, but when Dr Dearing is Chairman of the School Governors . . . It's just not on. They virtually had to eject Rabin from the premises. And I had to throw the rule book at him. You know," Chipmonk concluded, "if he'd lived, he could have become one of the worst sort of journalists. The objectionable foot-in-the-door type."

"A good investigator, then. Even if unpopular," Charlie Whyte prompted.

"That's right. Always delving into things. Whether he was wanted or not."

"Anything else he was working on that might have got him into trouble?"

"Let me see." The Deputy Head rummaged through the papers on his desk. "Nothing obvious," he replied. "Here's a record of the books he'd got out of the school library." He scanned the list. "A bit of fiction, environmental science, Stephen Hawking's *Time*, a history of the Channel Islands. That's probably a mistake. Sounds more like Rosalind Rabin's sort of thing. Anyway," he concluded, "nothing contentious."

"Okay," Detective Superintendent Whyte said. "When his records are assembled, I'd be grateful for a copy."

"No problem."

"Just one more thing," Charlie added. "You teach chemistry, don't you?"

"Combined science at GCSE, and A level chemistry, yes."

"Do you ever do experiments on cigarettes?"

"Cigarettes? No. Why?"

"Oh, I just wondered."

Chipmonk's curiosity was aroused. "What's this about?"

"Nothing to do with David Rabin, but as you're

a chemist, I thought I'd take the opportunity to ask. In one of my other cases I need an expert opinion."

"Oh, yes?" Chipmonk responded well to flattery. He liked being called an expert.

"We had occasion to raid a house. Found the usual drugs, you know. A right little den. But we also found quite a bit of nicotine. Odd."

"Very odd. It's pretty toxic. Same class of compound as strychnine."

"Yes," the policeman responded. "We want to know how it got there."

"And why?"

"Of course. Could it have been extracted from cigarettes, do you think?"

"I don't see why not," Chipmonk answered. "But . . . er . . . I think it occurs in tobacco as a complex, mainly."

"What?"

"Sorry. It's . . . in a different form. You'd have to convert it to free nicotine before isolating and purifying it."

"So, this would need special equipment?"

"Ideally, yes. But not necessarily. It could be done in a kitchen with a bit of fiddling about. Only you'd need some chemicals. Mind you, they're not specialized either. Acid, base and a solvent, that's probably all. You might get by with some cleaning fluid containing ammonia. Lemon juice or descaling fluid for the acid, and something like petrol as a solvent. Yes," he surmised, "it might be possible."

"Mmm. Interesting. Well, thanks for the advice."

"Of course," the schoolteacher continued, "if your crooks were chemists, they could just buy it. Cut out the fuss. The real question is," he mused, "why they had it."

"I've got our forensic people on to that one," Charlie said abruptly, clearly wishing to bring the session to an end. "Thanks again. I'll send someone for Rabin's records tomorrow. Okay?"

"Sure. You're welcome."

Back in his office, Charlie reviewed the findings of two officers on his team. One had interviewed Mr Smith who lived in the old caretaker's cottage, and the other had tried to make sense of Mr Edriss.

Mr Smith was retired. He spent his days collecting stamps and watching the activities at the school. He was particularly fond of whiling away the time on his patio that overlooked the field in which the body had been discovered. Mr Smith was in his seventies, but still reasonably healthy in body and mind. The kids at the school liked him because he always returned the balls that landed in his garden and he never blabbed to the teachers when he saw them sneaking out early. Voluntarily, he even acted as look-out for the school premises. He was known to Charlie because he'd once phoned the police station when he'd witnessed an attempted break-in at the school, from his bedroom window. On the night of David's death, he hadn't been so vigilant. He'd gone to bed at about eleven-thirty. Even if he had still been up, he wasn't in the habit of standing on his patio after dark, and his bedroom window overlooked the school, not the playing field.

Mr Edriss was younger, about fifty, and a different kettle of fish altogether. He hated children. Their noisy games on the field drove him to distraction. He would stand, hands on hips, at the end of his garden overlooking the field and try to intimidate the kids by his presence. He was grumpy and frequently shouted incoherent abuse until he broke down spluttering and coughing. Mr Edriss was an unpleasant eccentric. At one time he'd been employed by Dearing Scientific, but there had been an accidental spillage of some nasty chemical and he had been exposed to it. On the grounds of ill-health, he had taken early retirement with a considerable settlement from Dearings. Mr Edriss was also known to the police. Charlie still remembered the events that had ruined his Christmas eighteen months ago. It was Boxing Day. Charlie was hoping to spend a restful day with his family, when he got called out to take charge of the incident. It was Edriss's birthday on Boxing Day and he claimed that the local kids, out riding their new Christmas bikes and kicking new footballs on the school field, were disturbing him. His attempts to have a quiet birthday got out of hand. His verbal abuse directed at the boys became obscenities. Obscenities became physical abuse. The result was a boy with a torn jacket, bruised arm and cut lip. Mr Edriss was convicted on a charge of actual bodily harm. From that moment, he had ceased to be a laughing stock and became a menace.

The officer reported that Mr Edriss seemed delighted that there would be one less pupil at the school. No remorse whatever, and no alibi. Not even an attempt at a weak alibi. Wished he'd killed some of them himself ages ago. He had no qualms about being a suspect. In fact, he seemed proud to be considered a potential child murderer. A nasty piece of work. The notes ended with the observation that Mr Edriss was a chain-smoker. The entire output of a tobacco plantation was lying around his house.

Charlie Whyte slapped the progress reports back down on his desk. All his fears about the Rabin case seemed to be well founded. It *was* a funny one. And he still had a final interrogation to conduct. He'd kept the juiciest one for himself.

On his FAX machine, a message had come in from the forensic science laboratory. "Nicotine.

Found in dried leaves of *Nicotiana tabacum* and *Nicotiana rustica* at about 5% level, combined with various acids. Commercial nicotine available as by-product of tobacco industry. Simple extraction procedure given in several chemistry texts. It is a neuropoison; LD_{50} in rat for oral dose: 50 mg/kg. Symptoms of oral ingestion are extreme nausea, vomiting, mental confusion, uncontrolled bowel and bladder evacuation, convulsions. It has been used as a pesticide.

"Assuming the same LD_{50} in humans as in rats and given the victim's mass of 60 kg, a lethal dose would be about 3000 mg (3 g) by mouth.

"Regarding query about cigarettes, the average mass of tobacco in a cigarette is 650 mg, and about 5% of the mass is nicotine. Therefore, one cigarette would contain 32 mg nicotine. If extraction were complete the lethal oral dose for this victim would require nicotine from roughly 100 cigarettes. Given incomplete extraction and doubts about the precise lethal dose, a batch of 150–200 cigarettes would be more certain to give sufficient nicotine to cause death by oral ingestion."

Charlie didn't have a degree in maths or science but he understood the main thrust of the FAX message. Just ten packets of cigarettes, a bit of chemical knowledge, and someone could have concocted enough poison to kill a healthy young man. He sighed heavily. He felt depressed, intrigued and angry at the same time. Even after years of contact with crime, he had never quite gained immunity from the shock of the next grim finding.

The security guards in the reception at Dearings were expecting Mr Whyte. They had a visitor's badge ready and waiting for him. He was asked to wear it at all times when on the premises and to hand it in on his way out. On the site of Dearing Scientific, he was to be accompanied at all times and should not enter any buildings or rooms without the permission of a supervisor.

Within a few moments, a secretary arrived to escort him to Dr Dearing's office. On the way, Charlie asked her, "What exactly does Dearing Scientific do?"

The secretary smiled at him, but replied, "Oh, you'll have to ask Dr Dearing that. I'm just a secretary."

"I find," the policeman observed, "that secretaries know an awful lot. All those letters and memos that pass before you . . ."

"I don't understand most of it," she answered. "And besides, I don't talk about my job here. Not if I want to keep it." She pushed open a door to a lobby. "Take a seat," she invited him. "Dr Dearing will be with you any moment."

The Managing Director of the laboratories was a small man, about fifty years of age, and probably hyperactive. He shook the detective superintendent's hand firmly as if he was greeting a new customer rather than an investigator. "Come on in, come on in. Emma," he called to the secretary, "protect me from callers while I have Mr Whyte with me. And bring forward the Management Team meeting. I want them all here immediately after Mr Whyte's visit. Say, half an hour."

Charlie smiled to himself. Dr Dearing was attempting to take control of the timing of their interview.

When they were seated in his immaculately orderly office, Dr Dearing said, "Your people interviewed my security guards. Did it help? Could they tell you anything about this unfortunate incident?"

Maybe, by asking the first question, he was trying to dictate their whole session.

"No," Charlie replied. "Only that when it was light enough to pick out detail, David Rabin's foot was in view of one of your cameras. According to the time of death, he must have stumbled into that position between two-thirty and three a.m." In wresting back control of the interview, Charlie launched into his first question without hesitation. "Exactly what does Dearing Scientific do, Dr Dearing?"

"What has that got to do with your inquiries?"

"Look. A dead body is found yards from your premises. One of your staff discovered the body.

Naturally, I get curious about your business. In any investigation, the person who discovers a body is an immediate suspect. Usually, of course, they're rapidly eliminated from the inquiries. I'm here to find out if that applies in this case. So," he added before Dr Dearing could respond, "what is your business?"

"We undertake contract synthesis," the Director said unhelpfully.

"I'm not a scientist, Dr Dearing. Can you explain that?"

"We make the chemicals that people and organizations pay us to make."

"Like what?"

Dr Dearing laughed. "Mr Whyte. You may not be a scientist but, being in your profession, you'll appreciate the need for discretion in business. You can't expect me to reveal either our customers or their requirements."

"Okay, but what type of thing do you make for what type of customer?"

"Is this relevant?" Dr Dearing responded impatiently.

"Yes," Charlie affirmed. "David Rabin died from poisoning."

"Are you insinuating that the poison came from my laboratories?"

"No. But I would like to find out for sure. Have you come across strychnine?"

"Of course." Dr Dearing explained, "I am a chemist." As if to prove his knowledge, he continued, "It's a toxic alkaloid from the plant genus *Strychnos*, used as a poison for rodents. And in small amounts, it's used medicinally as a stimulant. But," he added, "if Rabin died from administration of strychnine, I hate to disappoint you, but we haven't handled it for years."

"So what type of thing do you handle for what type of customer?" Detective Superintendent Whyte repeated.

"A huge range. Some difficult-to-prepare starting materials that a customer – maybe a pharmaceutical company or a government research station – will use to make a desired end product. Sometimes we make the end product itself if the customer doesn't have appropriate labs or sufficient resources. If the product is a new drug, you'll understand the need for confidentiality. Someone's livelihood will depend on its patent and marketing."

"When you say the government," Charlie inquired, "do you mean the military?"

"The government has many different research stations, studying food, medicine, fisheries, and so on. It's not all military, you know," Dr Dearing growled. "I really can't say which ones we deal with."

Charlie tried a different approach. "What about nicotine?" he asked.

"Nicotine?"

"Yes."

"Another poisonous alkaloid. Yet it's all around us, thanks to smokers. We're fortunate that it's not more toxic than it actually is."

"Have you ever made it?"

"Why would anyone ask us to synthesize it?" Dr Dearing said. "One would simply buy it from a supplier. That's much cheaper than getting specialists like us to produce it."

"Do you keep any of it?"

"Possibly," Dr Dearing replied. "We have used it now and again as a starting material for making more complicated alkaloids. I suspect that we may still carry limited stocks. Why?"

Ignoring his question, Charlie asked, "Who has access to your stocks?"

The Managing Director shrugged. "Several of my chemists. But being a poison, they would have to requisition it. Notes are kept of all users." He paused then added, "I guess that you wish to have a copy of our usage of nicotine."

"I certainly do," Charlie said with some relish.

"I'll arrange that."

"Thanks. Does it go far back in time?"

"For as long as we've used nicotine."

"Do you think Mr Edriss might be on the list?"

"Edriss?" Dr Dearing looked surprised. "Now, there's a name from the past. Why do you ask?"

"Because I want to know. You remember your ex-employee?"

"Yes. But he was just a technician. Not scientific, you understand. He would fix things in labs, that's all. I'm not aware that he'd have any knowledge of chemicals. He might have picked up a bit as he went around, I suppose, but chemistry wasn't his job."

"So he won't be on your list of nicotine users."

"Certainly not."

"Do you keep in touch with him at all?" asked Charlie.

"No."

"Okay."

"Is that all?" asked Dr Dearing, looking at his watch. "Time presses."

The detective did not show any sign of leaving. "No," he said. "That's not quite all. You haven't mentioned your contact with the victim."

"Contact?"

"I have it that David Rabin came to this establishment on at least two occasions, some five weeks ago."

"Ah, yes. Indeed he did. An . . . unfortunate episode." Dr Dearing shuffled in his seat. "I applaud vigorous investigation of any project. It's the sound scientific method. He came here as part of an environmental project and, because I applaud initiative, I granted him a few minutes and sent him away with some literature on standard methods for containing dangerous chemicals." Dr Dearing sighed. "Apparently that wasn't enough for this particular boy. He came back, wanting specifics. You know – what we make, waste disposal procedures, effect on local rivers. I refused to see him, and the security guards escorted him from the site. There's a point where curiosity becomes . . . irksome, as I have indicated to you, Detective Superintendent."

"Mmm." Charlie was wondering if curiosity had killed the cat. "As far as you know, he didn't come back again?"

"Indeed not."

The policeman could easily envisage David Rabin attempting to gain entry to the laboratories on the night of his death. It seemed an extreme step for a school project, but maybe the lad thought he had learned something sinister about Dearing Scientific and was determined to follow it up.

"Okay," Charlie said, this time rising from his seat. "I'll need to send some of my people to talk to everyone present on this site on the night of the murder."

"But," the Director objected, "you've already spoken to the guards."

"I understand," Charlie returned, "that scientists are in the habit of always checking preliminary results. So am I."

Dr Dearing smiled faintly. "Yes. So you're not so ignorant of the scientific method as you made out."

"And, of course," the policeman continued, "there's the matter of any staff who have used your stocks of nicotine. I'll have them interviewed."

"Given your interest in nicotine, I assume that your comments about strychnine were designed to test my reaction to an irrelevant poison in this sorry affair. A red herring. Do I gather than *I* am a suspect?" His tone suggested that his good name should be beyond question.

"As you commented correctly earlier," Detective Superintendent Whyte responded, "in my business too, discretion is a blessing."

The detective left Dearing Scientific, feeling unfulfilled. He had on his hands a gruesome crime, plenty of suspects and several possible motives. Yet he had no obvious front-runner. His investigation had not so much hit a brick wall as opened up too many avenues to explore. There was the school chemistry teacher and the dreadful Mr Edriss. The connection with Dearing Scientific, though, was a particularly strong one. He could well imagine how an intruder to the site might be tied to a chair while the security breach was assessed. But force-feeding him a poison was the act of a sick mind. Of course, if there was something sinister about Dearings and Rabin, with his investigative instinct, had stumbled across it, then an over-zealous and over-protective worker might dream up a warped punishment. It was even possible that an ex-worker or sympathetic teacher might be paid to carry out the punishment. Maybe the nicotine was meant only to make him ill and the penalty was supposed to be nausea, not death.

Driving back to headquarters, Charlie's thoughts turned to Ros Rabin and Kevin Kingsnorth. Kevin's alibi had checked out. His two friends swore that the three of them had watched TV together till the early hours. Tracey, who had questioned them and who had a good nose for cock-and-bull stories, was convinced that they were lying. So, Kevin had primed them well. To prepare such a story, Kevin must have been tipped off about Charlie's interview with him. "Ros," the policeman muttered to himself. "She must have warned him I was on my way. The two of them in league. Sinister theories involving laboratories are all right as far as they go, but I like the tried and tested motives. An argument over a girl." True, Kevin Kingsnorth's tobacconist couldn't remember his buying a large stock of cigarettes, but there were plenty of other shops. And, as Tracey had noted, there was no rum among the small collection of bottles in one corner of Kevin Kingsnorth's living room. If he were the culprit, he would have ditched the bottle of rum. "Yes," Charlie mumbled, "the simple theories are still the best."

10

Kevin stepped into the Rabins' house for the first time and stood agog in the hall.

Ros shut the door, then said, "Are you okay, Kev?"

"Yeah," he answered. "It's just . . . so big. You could fit most of our house into this hall."

Ros laughed. "It's not that big. You're exaggerating."

"But what do you do with all this space? Just a small family and an enormous . . ." Kevin stopped talking when he saw the hurt expression on Ros's face. "Oops! Put my foot in it again. I didn't mean . . ."

"It's all right," Ros said. She sighed and muttered, "We *are* a small family. Just that I'm sensitive to being reminded of it." She tossed her hair over her shoulder, pretending she could cast aside her cares just as easily. "Come on. Let's get it over with."

Kevin did not follow her immediately. "What about your mum? Will she mind us messing around in David's room?"

"I dare say she would," Ros replied. "But she's out of it. Knocked out by the tablets. You could ride your motorbike round the house and she wouldn't notice. So she can't be hurt because she won't know about it. We'll just have to leave his bedroom tidy afterwards, in case she's well enough to get up and wander in later."

In his own place, the stairs up to the meagre bedrooms were narrow and steep, as if they had been squeezed in by the builders as an after-thought. In Ros's house, the stairs were wide and plush, built to be a lavish feature of the hall. Kevin didn't see the beauty, only extravagance, but he kept quiet for fear of upsetting Ros even more.

"Let's check out that photo first," he suggested.

"Okay. It's in my room."

They sat together on her bed and pored over the photograph of Ros's grandmother.

Kevin pointed to the striped pyjamas and asked, "This stuff was all the rage in those days, was it?"

"I don't know. It looks like fashion wasn't upper-most in her mind."

"You mean, she looks . . ." Kevin didn't want to offend Ros again so he didn't finish his sentence.

"Haggard's the word you're looking for," Ros said.

"Yes. Something like that. Where was it taken?"

"I'm not sure. Alderney, I guess."

"Alderney?"

"Yes." Ros explained. "My family used to live in the Channel Islands. Went there from France."

"You're French?"

Ros smiled. "No. But Grandmother and Grandfather were. After the war, Grandfather settled in the south – with Father, of course. They moved around a bit. A restless bunch, us Rabins. It's like Grandfather and Father were looking for somewhere, or something. But if they were, I was never told what it was, and I suppose they never found it. Anyway," she added, "we're as British as they come now."

Kevin took the photograph and turned it over. On the back, some writing was scrawled. They read, "Subject: Rabin 168/EAS. Twins eight days later. Mother did not survive."

"What's that mean?" Kevin asked, turning towards Ros. "Some sort of hospital code?"

Her face drained of colour, Ros stared at the writing. After a while, when she could speak again, she uttered, "Twins!"

"That's what it says." Kevin looked in her face,

then asked, "Didn't you know? You've got an uncle."

"No," she stammered. "No one told me."

"Didn't you see the writing the other night?"

"I didn't think to look on the back," she explained. Then she murmured, "An uncle! Why didn't they tell me? Is he alive?"

Kevin shrugged. "You'd better ask your mum. She'd know. At least, I guess she would."

"Yes," Ros replied. "When she's better, I will." Then, looking at her watch, she added, "That reminds me, I've got to give her her next lot of medicine. You stay here, I won't be long. I just wish I could . . ."

"Ask her about this uncle?" Kevin suggested.

"Yes."

"Why don't you try?"

"I've asked her a few questions. Like, what she wants to eat. No answer, or just nonsense. It's the shock, the doctor says, and the pills. It's no use asking her anything." Ros trudged out of the room, shouldering a new burden.

Kevin could not restrain his curiosity for the five minutes that Ros spent with her mother. Getting up from the bed he strolled around her bedroom. On her dressing table there were photographs of David and what he took to be her mother and father in happier days. The photographs were not prominently displayed. They probably signified respect more than sentimentality. Her make-up looked expensive and trendy – not tested on animals. Her various sprays were ozone friendly. She had her own compact disc player, and shelves laden with books – and not just cheap and tatty paperbacks. She had a desk, littered with school files and pens. Kevin flicked open one of the files and read the title: "The Controversy of Animal Experiments". He groaned and let go of the cover so that it flopped back into place.

There were no posters on her walls or door, but a decorative rug, made of loosely woven coloured twine, hung from the wall over her bed. When he turned round, he noticed an upright chair with a cord stretched across its back. From this main cord dangled knotted chains of multicoloured threads, like washing from a clothes line. Just as Kevin bent down to examine it closely, Ros came back in. "What's this?" he asked her.

"Macramé," she replied.

"What?"

"The craft of making decorative knots from cord. I use the back of a chair as a support. You can make screens or holders for plant pots. That one's destined to be another wall hanging – like the one over the bed."

"I didn't know you did that sort of thing. Very arty, I'm sure."

"Not your sort of thing," said Ros, "but I enjoy it."

"Each to his own," Kevin replied. "How's your mum?"

"The same."

"What about the family business?" Kevin queried. "While you're under eighteen and your mum's . . . as she is, who's handling it all?"

"We've got an accountant to look after it, so I don't have to worry. Anyway," she added, "let's get this other business over with. It's bugging me."

"Why's that?"

Ros shrugged. As she led the way along the landing towards David's room, she said, "I suppose it's because I feel like a vulture, picking over his remains." She shivered. "It doesn't seem right, somehow."

"We're not the only ones," Kevin reminded her as they went into the bedroom. "The police have been through his stuff already."

Standing in the middle of the room, Ros spread her arms. "Exactly! So what are we going to find that they couldn't?"

"No idea," Kevin replied. "We have to hope that we recognize it when we see it. Something . . . out of place. Something that's not right for David, maybe. You'd be better at that than the cops. You knew him. Perhaps there'll be something about this mystery uncle. Bet the law doesn't know about that, either."

"I doubt it," Ros muttered unhopefully.

"At least it's something else we know that the cops probably don't. Anyway," Kevin prompted, "let's get started." He pointed to David's illuminated tank where tropical fish glided sedately. "You don't think they'll tell us anything, do you?"

Ros managed a wry smile. "I wonder if they miss him."

"What? Fish?"

"I don't suppose they care as long as someone feeds them. I do it now. Do you think they notice the difference?" She didn't expect an answer. She paused, then continued, "He used to sit in the dark – just the light of the aquarium – listening to a CD, and watch the fish. Relaxed him, I think." She breathed deeply and shook her head. "You know, you shouldn't think too badly of him. He had a lot on his plate. The family to look after. And he was well-meaning. All this protecting me. Just that he went about it the wrong way. He only wanted the best for me, and for the family."

"And I wasn't the best," Kevin remarked.

"In David's eyes, no. I'm afraid not. But," she added, "I didn't share his view."

"I hope not."

"Let's get on with . . . this rotten job."

"Okay," Kevin agreed. "Just a thought. He didn't keep a diary, did he?"

"No, not as far as I know. And if he did," she answered, "the police would've taken it."

"Yeah. Guess so. What about the computer?" Kevin nodded towards the desk where the keyboard and monitor gathered dust. "Any info on it?"

"The police took all the disks to check. He used it for business and school projects, I think."

"Okay," he replied. "Keep your eyes open for a disk hidden somewhere. You never know." To Kevin, a computer was either a game or a device used by the rich to conduct a dishonest day's work. No honest sweat involved – not like digging, driving or decorating. In comparison, working with computers was hardly work at all. It occurred to Kevin that someone like David Rabin might have turned naturally to his computer if he had wanted to conceal a clue.

There was not a lot of data stored on the computer's hard disk, but they did find a section of a school report on an environmental project. Entitled "Disposal of Chemical Waste", it outlined David's discontent with the bland information given to him by Dearing Scientific.

"Interesting," Kevin murmured after he had read the section. "Might be worth bearing in mind. He was found near Dearings, as well."

"You don't think. . . ?"

Kevin interrupted her. "You never know. It's a dodgy set-up. Not to be trusted. Did David push his luck too far with them? Was he trying to break in?"

"David?" Ros exclaimed. More calmly, she added, "It doesn't sound like him."

"Perhaps not, but . . . maybe I'll check it out. Anyway, let's crack on."

His wardrobe and drawers revealed nothing more than the sort of dress sense that only the well-off can afford to have.

Tiring, Ros sighed. "It still doesn't feel right," she said. "It's like sacrilege."

"Even Tutankhamun probably wouldn't have cursed someone taking a gander around his tomb then replacing everything. We're not doing anything wrong. We're trying to help him – by getting to the bottom of it. Come on, Ros." He squeezed her arm. "Not much left. Don't give up now. Help me with his books and stuff, then it's all over."

Fiction, non-fiction, school books, magazines. "It's like his personal library," Kevin remarked.

"Mmm." Ros had picked up one book and, frowning, was flicking through its pages. "Now this is a bit odd," she said.

"Yes?" Kevin's ears pricked up. "Why? What is it?"

"History of the Channel Islands," Ros answered. "From the school library."

"So?"

"Well," she explained, "history wasn't really his thing. Economics, science, management – yes. But not history. And I can't see that he'd have any school work on it."

"Well," Kevin pondered, "perhaps it's something to do with the family. Interest in the background. You said your lot lived there once."

"Yes. Perhaps you're right," she said hesitantly. "If so, it's a recent interest."

"Keep the book," Kevin suggested. "You can go through it in case he's made any notes in it or marked something."

"Okay," Ros agreed, closing it. "I'll do that."

"I hope it tells us something," Kevin said, "because it's about all we've got. One lousy book. Still, it had to be done."

Before she left, Ros checked the room carefully. She wanted it left exactly as they'd found it – as if David himself might inspect it for signs of interference. When she was happy that it appeared undisturbed, she pulled the door closed, like sliding the lid over his coffin.

Back in Ros's room, she asked Kevin, "What now? Any ideas?"

"Yeah. Some," he replied. "I reckon I should ask around at school. I know the cops have been putting their snouts in already, but the kids'll talk to me. They'll tell me things they wouldn't dream of telling the law."

"You think someone might know something?"

"Well, I'll give it a whirl and report back," Kevin

replied. "Someone might just have seen something or heard something. But, for now," he added, "why don't you take me out for a drink?"

Ros hesitated. "I . . . I don't know. There's Mother."

"Ah, yes. Mother," Kevin responded, almost mockingly. "David's ghost and David's mother. Between them, they've trapped you."

"Up to a point, they have," Ros replied wilfully. "But there's no need to be like that about it. These things take time, that's all. I can't be seen out enjoying myself – not with things as they are."

"I suppose you're right." In a more conciliatory tone, he added, "I just get impatient – for it to be like it was."

She kissed him lightly, like a sister kisses a brother. "Won't be long," she said. "I promise."

On his way home, Kevin stopped his bike some distance from the school then walked quietly the rest of the way to the playing field. It was a warm, damp night. He vaulted over the railings and on to the playing field. The school buildings were dark, but lights still shone in some of the homes at the edge of the field. Mr Smith's lounge and one of the bedrooms in Mr Edriss's house were lit. The blank wall at the far side of the field hid any activity at Dearing Scientific.

Kevin made straight for the spot where David

had been found, careful to keep out of range of the security cameras. "David was poisoned," Kevin said to himself. "And behind this wall there's plenty of poisonous chemicals."

Kevin scrutinized the wall. Perhaps four metres high. Not easy to get over. Even with a good jump, outstretched fingers wouldn't reach the top. Besides, it was protected by sharp projections. But the spikes, Kevin decided, were also a weakness. It shouldn't be difficult to lasso one of them with a rope or cord and then scale the wall hand over fist. Rope-climbing to the top of the wall wouldn't have been beyond David, either. Of course, the cameras would be a problem. Or maybe not, if the night were dark and the climber avoided the best-lit sections of the wall. The drop on the other side would be ferocious but, if someone were really determined to break in to Dearings, it would be worth the risk. "Yes," Kevin muttered. "With rope, it would be possible. Worth checking out."

He turned and walked back across the field. When he drew level with Mr Smith's garden, the old man called to him, "Good evening, young man!"

Kevin started but, when he realized who had spoken, he replied cheerfully, "Hello."

"It's Kevin, isn't it?"

"Yes." Kevin strode to Mr Smith's fence. "What are you doing out at this hour?" he asked.

"Oh, just locking up the shed before I turn in," Mr Smith answered. "I could, of course, ask the same of you."

Kevin smiled. "That's true. I've just been over the field where . . . you know. Call it curiosity, if you like."

"Morbid curiosity."

"I guess so. Funny business, though, isn't it?" Kevin said. "A poisoning on our field."

"Poisoned, was he?"

"So the police say."

"Now, how'd a rogue like you know that? You haven't been in trouble again, have you?"

"No. But you know me, Mr Smith. Seem to attract the law's attention for no reason at all."

Once, when Kevin was dashing out of the school gates, he'd bumped into Mr Smith. He'd apologized, picked up the spilled shopping and carried it into his bungalow for him. Ever since, they'd struck up a casual friendship. Mr Smith seemed to enjoy Kevin's occasional visits. He was particularly fond of recounting his own childhood pranks and comparing them with Kevin's modern misdeeds.

"What you mean, young man, is that they suspect you of this terrible crime."

Kevin shrugged. "Yes. They know I had a row with him just before he copped it. The evidence was a black eye, I'm afraid."

The old man looked sternly at Kevin and asked, "Did you do it?"

"No."

"Mmm. You'll be fine, then. Nothing to worry about."

"I hope not. But I've decided to do a bit of investigating myself. See if I can turn up something."

"You be careful, my boy," warned Mr Smith.

"I can look after myself."

"Yes, I know." Mr Smith stretched his back and groaned a little. "Anyway, time for me to call it a day. Past my bedtime. Come and see me soon, when you have time off from your investigations. I'll make you a decent mug of coffee."

"Okay," Kevin replied. "I'll do that."

The old man shuffled away and Kevin headed back towards his bike. By the time he'd ridden home, got a bite to eat, found some rope, and walked back, he expected that everyone would have retired to bed. He could test his theory that it would have been possible for David Rabin to scale Dearings' wall unseen.

11

The dustbin lid in Mr Edriss's garden clattered on to the paving stones. Inside the house, Mr Edriss opened his bleary eyes and cursed. "Damn cats!" He clambered out of bed and staggered to the window. Drawing back the curtain, he squinted to see in the dark. At the end of his garden he could just make out a figure, grovelling on the ground. "That's no cat," he exclaimed. "Blooming kids!"

He struggled to free the latch on the window then push it open. "Oi!" he yelled at the top of his voice. "What do you think you're doing on my property?"

Clutching a torch in his hand the intruder straightened up, glanced towards the house, then made for the gate. Hurriedly, he slipped through and into the school field.

Mr Edriss called after him, "Don't trespass on my property again. I'll be watching!"

He closed the window and went back to bed, still muttering curses.

Once Mr Edriss had settled down again, the calm of night was restored. The daytime drone from the distant motorway had faded away. No cars cruised along School Lane. There was barely a breath of wind. Overhead, faint flashing lights marked the position of an aeroplane flying too high for its engines to be heard. Beyond, a thin screen of cloud muddied the moon.

Kevin stood, rope over his shoulder, looking alternately at his watch and at one of Dearings' security cameras that swivelled slowly like an owl's head, scanning back and forth. From its starting point, surveying the wall, the camera panned over a sector of the field, stopped, and swivelled back again in just two minutes. Anyone by the wall, Kevin guessed, would be out of shot for about one and a half minutes while the camera executed its scan of the field. It wasn't long. But was it long enough to throw and secure the rope, then mount the wall? He doubted it. Not unless the lasso found its target on the first attempt, which was unlikely. Kevin had never been blessed with good luck before, so he did not expect it now.

He planned to dash to the wall as soon as the camera began its outward sweep. Out of its field of view, he would fling the rope over one of the projections set into the top of the wall. Unless the rope caught first time, he wouldn't attempt to climb up within the same camera pan. He'd withdraw, trusting that on a dark night the lens would not pick out the dangling rope. Once the security camera had turned away again, he'd sprint back to the wall and mount it rapidly by pulling himself up with the rope.

As he waited for the right moment, he checked the loop that he had already made in the rope. He tested the strength of the knot by yanking on it. It held firm. When the camera began tracking to the right, Kevin raced to the wall and, keeping hold of one end of the rope, threw the other to the top of the wall. He expected the rope to slither down the wall and collapse in a heap at his feet, but it didn't. Amazed and delighted, he pulled on the rope to check that it had found its mark on the first attempt. For a while, it held. But when he put his weight on it, there was a wrenching noise and the rope went slack. One of the metal spikes clattered down the wall and struck him on the shoulder.

"Ouch!" he yelped.

The sharp metal had torn his jacket and possibly also his skin. He swore under his breath at the pain.

He glanced up at the camera. It had reached its outermost position and was beginning to swing back towards him. The urgency made him forget his injured shoulder for a while. He took the rope again and hurled it upwards. This time the lasso did not catch anything firm and the rope fell back around him.

Leaving the rope in a heap on the ground, Kevin dashed away from the spot before he found himself in camera shot. His heart beating strongly and rapidly, he rubbed his shoulder and waited. He was still determined to prove that David Rabin could have got into Dearing Scientific by this route. He had to succeed. It was the first step in proving that Rabin met his death inside these creepy laboratories.

Kevin's early confidence began to slip away when, on the next sweep of the camera, his four attempts to secure the rope all failed. Frustrated, he stood in the field getting his breath back. Suddenly, his throbbing shoulder suggested a different strategy.

When the camera next allowed, he sprinted back to the wall and dropped on to his hands and knees. Desperately, he searched for the metal spike that he had dislodged accidentally from the brick wall. When his hand stumbled across it, he grabbed it and, with the rope in his other hand, he withdrew. Sitting on the cold grass, he tied the long strip of metal securely to the end of his rope. He hoped that he could make the spike act like an anchor by lodging it between other projections on the wall.

The camera swung away and Kevin dashed in with renewed spirit. He flung the end of the rope, now heavy with the weight of his anchor, to the top of the wall. It crashed against something, making him wince at the noise, then plummeted down. Kevin side-stepped to avoid being struck again. He glanced at the position of the camera and tried again. This time, the rope did not end up at his feet. The spike had become wedged. He tested its grip by pulling with all his might on the rope but it remained firmly fixed. Kevin smiled. He was sure that it would take his weight. As long as the noise had gone unnoticed and the rope did not show up on the video, he was as good as in the Dearing Scientific compound.

He took a good, last look round the field to make sure that he had not attracted any attention, then dashed back to the wall. He jumped up, grabbed the rope with both hands and let out a cry of pain. In his excitement, he'd forgotten his damaged shoulder. The strain of heaving on the rope triggered pangs down his left arm. Resisting the temptation to let go, instead he tried to take more of his weight on his legs as he planted his feet against the brickwork. Groaning, he clambered up the wall, one step at a time, by yanking on the rope.

When his hands drew level with the top of the wall, he grabbed hold, keeping clear of the spikes, and scrambled up. The wall was not thick, but there was enough width to stand on without losing his balance. He glanced round briefly, noting that the camera would soon be taking pictures of his feet. He gulped when he saw the drop on the other side. He could jump, but there was a good chance that he'd break a leg.

Quickly, he squatted down, drew up the rope and let it down on the Dearing side of the wall. He adjusted the position of the spike to provide an anchor for the descent. Just before the camera caught him, he clutched the rope, let his legs drop down and, trying to ignore the agony of his shoulder, abseiled into Dearing Scientific's premises.

When his feet contacted the ground, he let go of the rope and crouched down. Automatically, his right hand felt his tender shoulder. He leaned against the wall for a few minutes, waiting to see if his entrance had gone unnoticed. He found himself on a narrow perimeter road. On the other side there was a building, made sinister by being in darkness. Further along the road there was another block. This one was brightly lit and, through its windows, Kevin could see that it contained laboratories.

No one came to arrest him. All was uncannily quiet. Kevin had proved his point: David could have slipped into Dearing Scientific to investigate their dubious operations.

Kevin stood up, then crept towards the laboratory building. He wanted to have a close look through one of the windows. If David had unearthed something corrupt before he'd been poisoned and his body dumped outside, perhaps Kevin could spot it as well. Perhaps Kevin could take David Rabin's place in exposing it.

Furtively, he continued along the road, keeping to the darker side. Just in front of the laboratories, a hedgehog shambled across the road, oblivious to Kevin's intrusion. Ignoring the animal, Kevin darted across the road and crouched for a while under one of the laboratory windows. Summoning up his courage, he raised his head slowly to peer into the room. There was movement in the lab but, eerily, it was empty of workers. To the right, a machine was shaking some flasks with yellow liquid inside. To the left, a robotic arm grabbed a syringe, filled it from a nearby vial then injected the liquid into some machine. By its side, a printer was churning out sheets of paper. Kevin was too far away to see what was written on them. He shuffled along the wall of the laboratories to get a closer look through the next window. At the top of one of the sheets he read, "ALKALOID DS5324. Average synthetic yield: 47%. Average biotechnological yield with tobacco enzyme: 61%."

"Tobacco," he murmured to himself. "Interesting." Thinking back to Detective Superintendent Whyte's strange questions about smoking, he whispered, "No way that's coincidence."

He sidled along the building to get a good view of the hard copy issuing from another printer, but before he reached the next window, he was stunned by a sudden dazzle. He froze, like a rabbit caught in a headlight beam.

"What. . . ?" he exclaimed.

He glanced down and, by the floodlighting, saw some sort of sensor attached to the base of the laboratory wall. His foot must have set it off. There was no audible alarm, but spotlights blazed threateningly. Kevin looked round but the guards had not yet appeared. It would not be long, he guessed. No time to run back and escape over the wall.

He sprinted down the road, located the hedgehog and, ignoring the prickles, picked it up. He raced back to the sensor and dumped the frightened animal right in front of it. Then he dashed around the corner of the laboratories out of the glare of the lights. Just a few metres away, he found the fire exit of the building and, with a sigh of relief, huddled in its gloomy recess.

He didn't have to wait for long. He soon heard the heavy footsteps of three, perhaps four, guards as they ran to the scene of the break-in.

They trampled about for a while, then Kevin heard one of them report to the others, "Here he is! Our culprit. It's a hedgehog. Walked through the infrared beam. Poor thing's petrified."

"Great! Let's get back. My coffee's getting cold."

"No," another guard called. "Spread out and double-check. Just in case."

Kevin cursed under his breath. His diversionary tactic had not succeeded. His heart thumped in his chest when he caught the sound of one of the officers walking round the corner of the labs. He must only be a few strides away. His torchlight flashed here and there, probing the darkness. Kevin drew himself as far into the recess as he could.

Just as the man drew level and threatened to turn and point his torch directly into the fire exit, another guard called from some distance away, "Here! I've found something!"

The man near Kevin disappeared back on to the perimeter road. But any relief that Kevin felt was short-lived. The first guard yelled, "I doubt if that hedgehog came over the wall by a rope!"

Kevin groaned. By discovering his rope, the enemy had cut off his retreat. Without an escape route, it was only a matter of time before he was ferreted out. Then what would happen to him? He wondered if David Rabin had been trapped in the same way. Was he now re-living Rabin's last few hours? The thought made him shudder.

He had no wish to cower in the doorway until he was cornered by the guards, but his exit over the wall had been blocked. He knew of only one other way out – the official one, by the gatehouse. It struck him that all of the security officers could be out searching for him, leaving the gatehouse unmanned. It was, he decided, worth a try. He'd never been inside the Dearings precinct before but knew that the exit must be along the perimeter road to the right, perhaps no more than a hundred metres away. He wished that he had Ros's speed but, even without it, he needed a burst of strength for just a few seconds. And, of course, a bit of luck. A sprint, a jump over the barrier, and freedom.

He stood upright and took three deep breaths. He accelerated out of the doorway like a greyhound from a trap, turned the corner on to the perimeter road, and immediately crashed into one of the security guards.

"What's this?" the man uttered as he spun round and expertly put an arm lock on Kevin. "Got him!" he called to his colleagues.

Kevin grimaced at the pain in his arm and shoulder.

As they converged on him, one guard said, "We caught ourselves a young one."

"What are you doing here, sonny? Come to get your ball back?" The voice was heavy with irony.

"No," Kevin replied. "I was out walking my pet hedgehog."

"Very funny," the chief officer retorted. "Come on. Back to base. Bring him." As an afterthought he said, "Jim, you stay and double-check – in case he came with a mate or has done any mischief."

Kevin was frogmarched down the road and into the security office. He was shoved roughly into a seat. His head hit the back of the chair and he yelped, "Ow!"

The man who was carrying Kevin's length of rope said, "Sit there quietly and don't make a move. If you do, I'll tie you to the chair with this." He dangled the rope threateningly in front of Kevin.

"All right, Frank. Let me get to him." The chief officer leaned uncomfortably close to Kevin and barked, "What's your name?"

Kevin's answer came out automatically, without really thinking. "David Rabin," he said. He guessed that he did it to test the man's reaction.

The guard didn't seem to recognize the name – or at least he acted as if he did not know it. "Okay," he replied. "David Rabin." He drew up a chair and sat opposite his prisoner. "Now, while one of my officers phones for the police, why don't we have a chat? You can start by telling me why you were on our land."

"I did it for a bet."

"A bet?"

"A dare. Some of the lads said I couldn't do it – get over the wall. I said I could."

"So why did you go walkabout? Why not climb over and straight back?"

"I don't know. I just got carried away. While over here, why not have a look around? It's a mysterious place, you know, to us on the other side of the wall."

"Curiosity."

"Yes."

"Did you find it interesting, whatever you saw in the laboratories?"

Kevin shrugged. "Not really. Couldn't see much. It wouldn't mean anything to me, anyhow."

"You still at school, or working?"

"School."

"And what about your family? Any in the chemical industry?"

Kevin laughed. "No chance. Honest labourers, us."

"Sure?" the security officer asked. "The police will check what you say, remember."

"They can check all they like. I don't know anyone who does chemistry. Except the school science teacher."

"And who's that?"

"Chipmonk. Mr Monk."

"Ah, yes. The local school. Dr Dearing knows him, I'm sure."

"You think I'm some sort of industrial spy!" Kevin exclaimed. The notion seemed absurd.

"It had occurred to me," the man replied. "But there could be any one of a number of reasons for this bit of trespassing." His tone was still threatening.

"I've told you the reason."

"Yes." The word signified agreement but this man made it sound like disbelief. "Have you got a camera on you?"

"No. Search me if you like."

"Stand up," he ordered.

He ran his hands up Kevin's legs, feeling his pockets particularly, over his trunk and then down each arm in turn.

"He's clean," he said over Kevin's shoulder to his colleagues.

The man who had hold of the rope was scowling. "Kids!" he murmured. "We should teach him a lesson."

"We'll leave that to the police, Frank," the chief answered.

"If I had my way . . ." Frank began.

"Here they come!" a third guard said.

Kevin groaned when he saw who had rushed into the office. "Oh, it's you," he couldn't help saying.

Detective Superintendent Whyte frowned. "Who do you think it'd be when a message comes in that David Rabin's broken into Dearing Scientific?"

The senior security officer and Detective Superintendent Whyte went into a huddle for a few minutes to exchange information, then Kevin was led away.

In the back of the police car, Kevin faced yet more questions. "Why David Rabin? Why use his name?"

Kevin decided that there was no harm in telling the truth. "I wanted to see their reactions."

"Why?"

"Oh, come on. Bet you've checked out Dearings. This was my way of doing it."

"What was the reaction?"

"There wasn't one."

"And if there had been? What would it prove? That they'd read and remembered his name from newspaper reports. Big deal."

"Well, if one of them had turned bright red it would've told me something. There was one called Frank. He'd turned away when I said I was Rabin. Perhaps he turned red. I couldn't see his face."

"Why do you say that?"

"He seemed ... I don't know ... nasty. Threatened me."

"In what way?"

"You burst in before he got round to details. But he did threaten to tie me to the chair if I made any trouble."

"Oh yes?" the policeman put in, suddenly interested. "What sort of chair?"

Kevin shrugged. "An ordinary chair. Not an electric one."

Ignoring the joke, the policeman probed further. "Did it have a low back?"

"No. I hit my head on it at one stage."

"Mmm." Detective Superintendent Whyte said no more on the topic. Instead he asked, "Why did you do it, Kevin? Why go over the wall?"

"To show that David Rabin might have gone over that night. Hey!" Kevin said. "This isn't the way to the police station. Where are you taking me?"

"Home."

"Home?"

"What do I want to clutter the station with you for? You're not going to leave the country, are you? I can pick you up any time if I want to talk to you. Remember that, Kevin." The policeman glanced meaningfully at him. Then he added, "I've got all I need for a report. But if Dr Dearing wants it taken further, I'll pull you in again."

"Okay," Kevin replied defiantly. "But there's something else you should know. Dearings is working on tobacco."

"Tobacco? Now, why do you think I'd be interested in that?"

"Because you asked me about smoking. There's something about cigarettes in all this, isn't there?"

Detective Superintendent Whyte took no notice of his question. "What makes you believe they're working on tobacco?"

"I saw a print-out in one of the labs. Something about using a tobacco enzyme. Whatever that means." The car took a sharp left corner and Kevin swayed on the back seat, clutching his injured shoulder. He added, "You're interested, aren't you?"

"In a case like this, I'm interested in anything."

"Sure." Kevin smiled to himself. The night had been even more useful than he'd thought it would be. He was learning a lot. "There's another thing, as well," he said.

"Yes?"

"It shows I didn't do him in. If I had, I wouldn't be going to all this bother. I reckon they did it."

"They?"

"Someone at Dearings. Strange place. David Rabin was suspicious about it. He could have broken in. They've got plenty of poisons. And there's the smoking business that you won't tell me about. They could've stopped him making a nuisance of himself by poisoning him."

"And that's supposed to let you off the hook?"

"Sure it is."

"Your prank tonight," the policeman replied, "could be construed as the actions of the villain desperate to put the blame on someone else."

"That's daft," Kevin retorted. "Can't you see? It wasn't me. It was them."

"We'll see," the policeman replied. "The truth will out."

The car pulled into Curtis Street and cruised to a stop outside his house.

Kevin got out and, through the open door, tried his luck once more. "David Rabin was poisoned by something in ciggies, wasn't he?"

The policeman shrugged. "It's too early to be sure. I keep an open mind on such matters." He paused, then added, "Don't pull any more stunts like this one, Kingsnorth, or you *will* be in trouble. I won't need much excuse to drag you in and make things deeply unpleasant next time. Understand?"

Kevin smiled. "Thanks for the lift."

12

The kids in David Rabin's class had plenty of theories. "Rabin never did hit it off with old Chipmonk. And, him being the science teacher, he'd know all about poisoning. I reckon it was Chipmonk." It wasn't the first time that someone had accused the Deputy Head as Kevin strolled around the playground casually asking questions or listening to the rumours. "No doubt about it. Edriss did it. He hates us all. Love to get rid of us. Bet he did it." There were quiet mutterings too about Craig Blackstock. No one dared to say why, but one girl suggested that Kevin should see him if he wanted to know who else might bear David Rabin a grudge.

Not many in the school would volunteer to go

and see Craig Blackstock. Several were "invited" by his sidekicks to meet him at a certain time, in a certain place. Or Craig Blackstock might "interview" one of the children when he was least expected or wanted. Yet he had never sought out Kevin. He even had a degree of respect for Kevin – probably because he'd been in trouble with the law. Kevin didn't approve of the school bully, but he wasn't scared of him like everyone else.

When Kevin approached Craig Blackstock, he was flanked, as always, by two pals. "What is it, Kingsnorth?" he asked, adopting his usual tone which was meant to intimidate.

"The word is," Kevin said, "that you and Rabin had a . . . confrontation before he copped it."

"The word is, so did you."

"Yeah. I can't deny that. Everyone saw the punch-up."

"So," Craig Blackstock replied, "who says I had a go at him as well?"

"No one in particular. Just a rumour. All I want to know is, who else the cops might be investigating."

"Not me. No one'll tell them about me. Will they, Kingsnorth?" he added pointedly.

"You know I don't mix with the law. I won't say anything. But if they come back and ask around . . . you never know. Someone might let it out."

"Then I give them my alibi."

"What's that?"

"American football on the box that night."

"You too, eh?" Kevin couldn't help smiling.

"You mean, you've used that alibi?"

"'Fraid so. I got in first. They'll never believe the same thing from you."

"But I *was* watching it. Were you?"

Kevin shrugged. "Can't you dream up another alibi?"

"Perhaps I'd say I was watching it with you."

"I wouldn't do that. I've already told them who I watched it with. You can't get added to the list now. It's too late. Anyway," Kevin said to change the subject, "all this suggests you did have an . . . interview with Rabin."

"Yes, we had a little chat."

"What about?"

Craig Blackstock was built like a tank. And he had a business sense to match. Kevin knew what a little chat meant but he was hoping to learn more.

"I told him I'd heard that some of the lads were threatening to do him over. You know how enthusiastic some kids get for that sort of thing, especially with someone like Rabin. I told him I could help him out – stop the lads having a go at him – for a small fee."

Kevin nodded. It was much as he'd expected. "What did Rabin say?"

"You've got to give him credit. He told me where to get off."

"Really?"

"Yeah. Not many do that. Must've had a death wish. Judging by what happened, he did. Someone else gunning for him."

"It wasn't you, then?"

"It's not clever, or polite, even to think that." Craig Blackstock's minders each took a step towards Kevin. "I'd have had him the next day, of course. My reputation to think of. But I'd only have roughed him up and made sure everyone knew it was me. Anyway," he added, "I've had enough of this. Before you go too far, let's end this . . . meeting. I wouldn't want to have to teach you a lesson as well."

Kevin left. He felt that Blackstock was probably telling the truth. But everyone knew how he spent the money that he prised out of the weaker school-children. His ill-gotten gains funded his craving for cigarettes.

Ros's mother was propped up in bed, sipping some soup. She was pale and withdrawn. She would not speak unless Ros spoke to her, and then Ros had to repeat all her questions before she got a response. Her mother's eyes stared blankly when Ros asked about her missing uncle.

"Mother! This is important. Do I have an uncle? Where is he? Who is he?"

Her mother spilled some of her soup and fussed

over the mess to avoid answering the question. When Ros repeated it, she replied, "Uncle? You mean your father's brother?"

"Yes. Did he have a brother?"

"He . . . er . . . We don't talk about him."

"So I *do* have one! Why don't we talk about him?"

Mrs Rabin shook her head, utterly distraught. "We just don't."

"Why not?" Ros repeated.

"Because it's time we forgot about him."

"What do you mean?"

"Forget him."

"Why? Why have you never told me about him?"

"Don't you get involved, Ros. Leave it be. It's time we stopped living in the past."

Ros knew when to give up. Her mother had withdrawn into her shell of remorse. If Ros wanted to learn more, she'd have to find out for herself.

In her imagination, Ros could see a shadowy uncle, embittered by being cut out of the Rabin family for some unknown reason. Rejection had unhinged him. He was completely mad but, in Ros's eyes, he was also very sad. And he was now wreaking revenge on the family for being left out in the cold.

If it were true, if the Rabins were being stalked by a disgruntled and long-since-disowned relative, would he stop at David's murder? Was that enough to appease him? Or would he continue his vendetta until he alone survived and inherited the family's wealth?

One other thought troubled Ros. She wondered where honour lay – if there could be honour in such a family feud. Who were the heroes and who the villains? She dreaded the possibility that the Rabins might have committed an unforgivable wrong against her uncle. If they had, she would be counted as one of the bad guys. She didn't want to live the rest of her life with that on her conscience.

Before he died, David Rabin had been tied with cord to a chair with a high back. Following his escapade at Dearings, Kevin Kingsnorth claimed that one of the security guards had threatened to tie him to the same type of chair. Detective Superintendent Whyte was forced to give fresh credence to the involvement of Dearings in Rabin's death.

On Charlie's instructions, the forensic scientists had examined a couple of chairs from Dearing Scientific's security office for evidence of contact with David Rabin. Fresh from the FAX machine, the forensic report was disappointingly negative. No fibres from the victim's clothing had been found adhering to the chairs. The report concluded that it was most unlikely that David Rabin had been forced to sit in either of those particular chairs.

There was another explanation of Kevin's story. When the police checked it out, the guard whose name was Frank had denied all knowledge of the threat to tie up the intruder. It was possible that Kingsnorth had made up the whole story. If Kevin was guilty of Rabin's murder, he would have known that David Rabin's body bore the marks of being tied to a chair. He would have also known about the poisoning with nicotine. And he would want to deflect suspicion elsewhere. He could have broken into Dearings to invent the episode with the rope and the reference to tobacco in the laboratories. Very neat. He would have also known that industrial secrecy would prevent the police verifying his claim that the chemists were working with tobacco. He could make lots of allegations, knowing that they could not be checked. As long as they sounded real, Kingsnorth probably thought he could get away with it. He could make someone at Dearing Laboratories seem guilty and, at the same time, appear innocent himself.

Detective Superintendent Whyte knew that the lad was reckless. But was Kevin also sincere and blameless, or a cunning murderer? Charlie wasn't sure which, but he intended to find out. He decided to apply for a warrant to search Kingsnorth's house.

13

The spooky atmosphere of the deserted swimming pool was lost. Rain pelted down on the windows and the smell of disinfectant was too powerful to be pleasant. Somewhere, doors banged regularly, so Ros and Kevin kept thinking that their sanctuary was about to be invaded. Even so, they stayed long enough to compare notes.

When Kevin told her how he had spent the night, Ros shuddered. "You're playing with fire," she warned him.

Kevin smiled at her. "Yes," he replied. "Good, eh?"

He was right. Kevin could excite her and scare her at the same time. That was why she found him intriguing. Even so, she tried to express her doubts. "But the risk . . ."

"It was worth the risk," Kevin put in. "Just think what we learnt. David could have got into Dearings. I'm sure he was poisoned by something in cigarettes. And the law got all interested in me being tied up. I reckon David was tied to a chair at some point. Someone in those labs, maybe this character Frank, is my main suspect."

"But it's not certain.. There are others."

"Yeah, too many. There's Dr Dearing himself, Craig Blackstock and his crew, and Edriss. According to the kids in David's class, Chipmonk's a possibility. And," he went on, "if you believe the cops, there's you and me."

"Yes, I guess so. But this idea of Chipmonk. It rings a bell. David had a clash with him not long ago, I'm sure."

"What sort of clash? What do you mean?"

"An argument. Some report that Chipmonk wrote on David. It wasn't very . . . complimentary. You know, full of damning comments. David thought it had nothing to do with his ability. Just that Chipmonk was smarting over David's antics at Dearings. He seemed to be trying to get his own back. And David wasn't afraid to say so. You know David – not one to duck a confrontation. He took his case to the Head and managed to convince him that the comments weren't deserved. Chipmonk had to admit they were influenced by personal feelings and climb down. He was in a dreadful mood for at least a week after, David said."

Kevin nodded. "That sounds like Chipmonk. And that puts him right up there with the rest of our suspects. He bore David a grudge. But," Kevin asked, "how about you? Any joy with your mum?"

Ros reported her short conversation and added a mysterious uncle to their list of suspects. "But," she said, "the Channel Islands book didn't help. I checked every page but David respected books too much to scribble notes in them."

"Pity."

"I've started to read it, cover to cover. Just in case there's anything relevant in it. Can't think what it might be, though. So," she asked, "where do we go from here?"

"What have we got?" Kevin thought aloud. "Lots of suspects, lots of motives. Not much evidence. You reckon there's a Channel Islands connection, and David used that photo to point the finger at some missing uncle. I reckon cigarettes come into it. And there's the torch. We need to find that torch – preferably on someone who knows his tobacco chemistry."

"You're not thinking of going back into Dearing Scientific, are you?" Ros asked in alarm. "To look for the torch?" She put her hand on his shoulder as if she could hold him back.

He winced at her touch. "Ouch! My shoulder."

"Sorry." She took away her hand. "How is it?"

"Okay – till you wrecked it," he replied. Then he smiled and added, "No. It's all right. Strapped up."

"I thought you'd added a few inches. Padded shoulders."

"Anyway," he answered her, "I don't think I'd better go back – not yet. It's too soon. Too dangerous right now."

"So where do we search?"

Kevin shrugged. "I could do Edriss's place, some time when he's out. Or Chipmonk's. That'd be easier. I'll check his lab first. If he brewed up something in the lab, there might be some sign of it."

"You don't sound hopeful, though."

"I still think the answer's in Dearings," he said firmly. "Oh, I'm going to have a chat with Mr Smith, as well. You never know what he might have seen."

"Don't you think the police will have interviewed him already? And everyone else living round the field?"

"I guess so. But he'll talk to me as well – maybe more than he'll talk to the cops. He's all right, the old man. We get on okay."

Before they left the poolside they agreed that, after Kevin had seen Mr Smith, they would check out the school chemistry laboratory for clues together.

*　　*　　*

The door chimes didn't seem to work so Kevin banged on the glass of Mr Smith's front door. After a few minutes, the old man opened the door and his face lit up. "Ah, it's you, Kevin," he said.

"Well, you offered me a coffee the other night. I've come to collect."

Mr Smith laughed. "You're welcome, young man. Come on in."

Kevin pulled back from stepping inside when he saw an envelope on the floor. He bent down and picked it up. It was a small parcel addressed to Mr Edward A. Smith. "Here," he said, handing it to his host. "The postman's been."

"Oh, thank you." Mr Smith examined the package and murmured, "Good. I've been waiting for this. It's a packet of stamps. I collect them, you know. Fascinating."

"Yes. Fascinating." Kevin tried to sound fascinated.

"Heh, heh!" Mr Smith chuckled. "You don't have to pretend. To you, it's boring. But to me . . . Well, when you get to my age, you'll see the attraction. Nostalgia mainly. Anyway, come in. I'll go and put the coffee on."

As always, Kevin found Mr Smith's bungalow oppressively hot. As always, Mr Smith asked him if he was warm enough. "Yes. Sweltering, thanks." He took off his jacket.

"There's a cold wind today. Difficult to keep the place warm."

The dining room table was awash with stamps, albums, a magnifying glass, tweezers, catalogues and notes. Mr Smith carried a tray with two large steaming mugs towards the table but changed his mind when he saw the mess. "We'd better have these somewhere else."

They sat on either side of a coffee table by the patio door that overlooked the playing field. After a few minutes of conversation about the weather, Kevin nodded towards the field and said, "All happening out there these days."

"Has something else happened?" asked the old man.

"Not really." Kevin thought better of telling him about his assault on the Dearing precinct. "Just this murder. Did you know him? David Rabin."

"Yes and no. I've seen him around, I think. Coming and going. Usually on his own. A bit of a loner, if I'm any judge. I didn't know him by name but I recognized his picture in the papers. Poor lad." Mr Smith shook his head sadly. "So young."

"Yeah."

"But you said you'd been fighting with him, or something. Not a friend of yours?"

"We had an argument about a girl."

"A girl? At your age?" The old man frowned playfully. "Hope she was worth it."

"It was his sister." Kevin tasted the thick coffee, which acted on his throat like paint-stripper on aged gloss. "Phew! That's . . . good."

"Mmm. When the coffee's good, you've got to have it strong to really appreciate the flavour. None of that decaffeinated rubbish." He gulped his own as if it were a draught of cold water. "So," he went on, "what had you been doing to this poor lad's sister?"

"Nothing. I just didn't match up to expectations."

"You mean, she's posh."

Kevin smiled. "And I'm not."

"Where does she live?"

"A big place up Laburnum Avenue."

"Ah. And you?"

"Curtis Street."

Mr Smith nodded knowingly. "I see the problem."

"Well, the main problem's . . . dead and gone." Gingerly, Kevin swallowed a small amount of his coffee and then added, "Now there's the law on my back."

"If you didn't do it, Kevin, you'll be cleared, sooner or later."

"Maybe. But this Detective Superintendent Whyte's a swine. Got it in for me. Has he seen you?"

"Me?"

"Yes. In case you saw anything that night."

"No," Mr Smith replied. "Someone came, though. A policeman, but his name wasn't Whyte."

"What did he ask?"

Mr Smith shrugged. "Just when I'd gone to bed and if I'd seen anything suspicious. That sort of thing."

"And did you?"

"No. Not so's I'd notice."

"Anything unusual going on at Dearings about that time – or since?"

"I'd like to help you, young man, but . . ." He spread his hands in a gesture of futility. "You seem to think that Dearing place had something to do with it. You were looking at it the other night as well."

"It's possible, yes. They're into chemicals. Bet they've got all the poisons you could want."

"But what do the police think? Does this . . . Whyte suspect them as well?"

"I think so," Kevin answered, "but I reckon he's got me at the top of his list."

"As I said the other night," Mr Smith cautioned him, "you be careful."

Kevin heard the advice but didn't comment on it. Instead, he quizzed the old man again. "You said Rabin was usually on his own. Who was he with when he wasn't on his own?"

"I've seen him with that grumpy teacher. What's his name? The Deputy Head or something."

"Mr Monk, the science teacher?"

"Yes. That's him. They seemed to be bickering."

"Anyone else?"

"Yes. The day before he came to grief. I don't know names," said Mr Smith, "but he tangled with two or three boys. Right outside my garden. One of them was trying to talk to him but he wouldn't have it. The others went to grab him but he pushed them away and shot off. Good for him, getting out of trouble."

"Sounds like Craig Blackstock."

"Who?"

"The school bully."

"That may be so. The main boy had that sort of air about him."

Kevin drained his coffee mug and found himself biting on some grains that lay at the bottom like mud in a pond. "I wonder if you can do something for me," he said.

"I should think so," the old man replied. "As long as you don't want me to sneak about in the dead of night doing your investigations. I wouldn't be any good at that sort of thing," he chuckled.

"No, nothing like that," Kevin reassured him. "I just want you to keep an eye open. Especially if anything funny's going on over the field – in Dearings. Okay?"

Mr Smith smiled. "Yes, I can do that. I haven't got much to do but watch comings and goings anyway. Along with the stamps." He nodded towards the dining table.

"Thanks," Kevin replied. "You can wave to me as I go past, if you've got any news for me."

"Or I could phone. You're in the phone book, aren't you? Kingsnorth, isn't it?"

"Yes. We're in there."

Mr Smith looked very cheerful. Kevin thought that the old man had suddenly found a new purpose and relished the prospect of turning detective.

"And I'll do something for you in return," Kevin said. "I'll look out for stamps for you."

"Would you? I'm always grateful for them. It's something you should take up, you know. Stamp collecting. It's not so dangerous as investigating murders."

Kevin smiled. "I guess not. But ... er ... It doesn't turn on the girls. You don't hear them say, 'Cor, I really fancy Kev. He collects stamps, you know'."

"So that's why I've been short of female callers all these years."

Mr Smith was still chortling quietly as Kevin saw himself out of the cottage.

It was break-time at school when Ros and Kevin slipped in to the main chemistry lab when no one was looking.

"We're not allowed in here without a teacher,"

Kevin reminded her in a whisper, "so we'll have to be quiet. Keep a watch on the window as well, in case anyone looks in."

Ros was well aware that she was breaking the school rules. Her heart thumped and she had broken into a sweat. She'd decided to help Kevin only after much wrestling with her conscience. Kevin didn't expect to remain undisturbed for long in the laboratory, so he needed some help to search it quickly. In silence, they set about their task of looking for anything odd. They peered into each unlocked cupboard and tried each drawer, bench by bench.

They found nothing.

"Let's go," Ros urged.

"Let me just take a look at Chipmonk's stuff," Kevin breathed, determined not to miss anything.

As soon as he lifted the lid of Chipmonk's desk, he let out a gasp. "Bingo!" he said. "Over here."

Ros tiptoed to his side and glanced into the desk.

Lying on top of all his things, there was a chemistry book. Its title was *Tobacco Products*.

"Well, well," Kevin said quietly. "Whichever way I turn, the topic of the day is ciggies."

"There's a bookmark in it," Ros pointed out.

Kevin opened the book at the marked page. It was the beginning of a chapter on nicotine.

"Nicotine," Kevin murmured. "I wonder . . ."

Together they read, "Nicotine [3-(1-methyl-2-pyrrolidinyl)pyridine] is a colourless and highly toxic product obtained from dried tobacco leaves."

"Poisoned by nicotine," Kevin whispered to Ros. "It could be." He put the book down and began to rummage in the teacher's desk. "I wonder if there's any more incriminating evidence."

"Quickly, Kev," Ros urged, aware that Mr Monk could return at any moment. "And don't disturb it too much. If he knows someone's been rooting through his things . . ."

"He won't know it was us."

"But if he's . . . guilty, he'll try and find out. We could be skating on thin ice."

"Ah! It's worth it, though. Look."

Tucked between some laboratory notebooks and the side of the desk was a packet of cigarettes.

"Interesting. Especially because I'm sure he doesn't smoke himself," Kevin said, "but there's nothing else here. Let's get out."

Kevin poked his head round the door of the lab to check if the walkway outside was clear of teachers. He found himself peering at Mr Monk who was about to enter the laboratory.

"What do you think you're doing in there?" Chipmonk bellowed at him.

"Er . ."

The science teacher grabbed the door handle and

opened it fully. When he saw Ros, he seemed to calm down somewhat. "Rosalind Rabin. You as well. What's going on?"

"We . . . er . . . just came in to see if you were here." Ros tried to fib without blushing.

"Yeah." Kevin took over the explanation from her. "You weren't, so we were on our way out."

"You're not allowed in the laboratories under any circumstances without a teacher."

"I know," Kevin replied. "That's why we were leaving."

"What did you want to see me about?" asked Chipmonk.

"It was about David," Ros replied.

"David?"

"There's a couple of science books missing. The local library's been bothering us for them. We thought he might have left them in a locker or desk here."

Chipmonk didn't answer immediately. He peered at Ros, assessing her honesty. "No," he said eventually. "The police took all his effects from here. And I don't recall there being any such books."

"Oh," Ros said. "Okay. Thanks anyway."

Eyeing them both as they made for the door, the science teacher commented, "Remember, in future, the rules about entering laboratories."

"Yes. Sorry," Ros returned.

*　　*　　*

Outside, Ros sighed with relief.

"Quick thinking," Kevin congratulated her. "You'll make a rogue yet."

"Great! Just what I've always wanted."

Kevin smiled at her. "Never mind. At least we got what we wanted."

"What do you mean?"

"Evidence. Chipmonk's tobacco book and the fag packet."

"So," Ros asked in a whisper, "are you going to call the police?"

"No!" Kevin shook his head. "Not a hope. We need more evidence than that. He could have just confiscated the ciggies from some unlucky kid."

"What other evidence?"

"David's torch, or that plastic bag he was carrying. A half-used bottle labelled poison. That sort of thing."

"But even if Chipmonk did it, how are you going to find them? They weren't in the lab, as far as we could see."

Kevin shrugged. "Maybe I should find out where he lives."

"No," Ros replied sharply. "If he's . . . the one, it's too dangerous. He might suspect that we're on to him after that little affair." She pointed towards the science block.

"Mmm. True," Kevin replied. "But we need that torch – desperately."

He did not know then that David's torch was about to turn up – in the most unexpected place.

14

Detective Superintendent Whyte, bearing a search warrant and a businesslike frown, arrived at Kevin's door with Tracey and four other officers.

Kevin was taken aback. He hadn't expected the policeman to carry out his threat to search the house, but he couldn't prevent it, so he stood aside and put on a brave face. "It's only a small house, you know," he said. "No need to bring a complete squad."

"Last time I was here," Charlie replied menacingly, "you invited me to be thorough. We're going to be very thorough."

"I also said I was clean. I'm not scared," Kevin retorted. "Get on with it."

another offence, they'd really lay into him. But this time it was murder, not arson. They'd send him down for good.

"So," the detective superintendent asked as they sat down at the dinner table, "how do you account for the haul behind your shed? How did they get there?"

Kevin clutched at straws. "I guess someone must have planted them there."

"Why would anyone do that?"

"To make it seem as if I did it."

"Really?"

"Yes. How else could they have got there?" Kevin said defiantly.

"Don't get hot under the collar," the detective replied. "I happen to agree with you."

"What?" Kevin could hardly believe his ears.

"I agree with you."

"Really? You're not having me on?"

Charlie smiled for the first time. "No. Scouts' honour."

"Why?" asked Kevin.

"Because you're not that daft. If you'd concocted the poison, you'd have got rid of the evidence by now," said the policeman. "And, besides, those packets haven't been there that long. Plenty of cobwebs around but hardly any attached to the packets."

The relief was clear in Kevin's face. The threat of

a harsh and unjust punishment had faded. "So," he queried, "where do we go from here?"

"We? Well, you help me – by telling me what you know. Start with the torch behind your shed. What do you know about it?"

"Nothing for sure, but I guess it's David Rabin's." Helping the police didn't suit Kevin, yet he felt so relieved that he launched into the conversation without thinking about it. "Ros thinks he may have set out that night with a torch."

"Yes, that makes sense. We'll check it for his fingerprints. And for yours, of course. We'll still have them on file from your last offence. Now," he continued, "who'd want to pin his murder on you? Who have you upset recently?"

"Well, it could be someone at ... No, it couldn't."

"Who were you going to suggest? Someone at Dearings?"

"Yes, but I told them I was David Rabin, so they couldn't have traced me here." He looked into the policeman's thoughtful face and added, "Unless . . ."

"Unless I told them who you were," Charlie spoke for him. "You see," he explained, "when Dr Dearing heard about your escapade, he was intrigued by a visitation from beyond the grave. He knew David Rabin, remember."

"So he found out from you who I was?"

"I'm afraid so," the policeman confessed. "It's interesting, though, isn't it? They find out it's you and almost immediately, some evidence turns up here."

"Yes, very interesting. I told you so – in the car that night."

"Let's not jump to hasty conclusions," the detective superintendent said. "Is there anyone else who might have committed the murder and who'd like you to carry the can?"

"Possibly."

"Who?"

"Well, there's Mr Monk at school." Kevin recounted how the Deputy Head had caught him and Ros in his laboratory. He also mentioned that Chipmonk had cigarettes and a book on tobacco in his desk. "And he'd easily be able to look up where I live. Pretty suspicious, eh?" he concluded.

"Not necessarily," Charlie replied. "I talked to him about nicotine at one stage. Perhaps I aroused his curiosity enough to consult a book or try out a few experiments. Still," he added, "I'll bear it in mind. Have you confronted anyone else who'd know your address? How about that crackpot, Edriss?"

"No. Haven't been near him."

"Who else, then? At school, perhaps?"

"Well, just about anybody there would know where I live."

"But are there any particular kids who are crazy

enough to get involved in a case of poisoning?" the detective pressed him.

Kevin hesitated. He was getting perilously close to being a sneak.

"What about Craig Blackstock?" Charlie prompted.

"Why him?"

"Oh, we've made inquiries at school. Quite a bully, that lad. And I heard a whisper that he'd had a disagreement with Rabin. Is that true?"

"I don't know. It might be."

"So, did you confront Craig Blackstock?"

Kevin wasn't sure why he was unwilling to incriminate such a boy. He was a nasty piece of work, and if he was a killer, he could be a threat to Kevin. "I . . . er . . . had a brief word with him, I think," Kevin said.

"You think. That's good enough for me. Have you got on the wrong side of any others over the Rabin business?"

"I don't think so," Kevin answered.

"Okay," Charlie said. "I believe you. You've been quite helpful. I can only think of two other possibilities."

"Oh? Like what?"

"You really want to know?"

"Yes."

"Ros Rabin might want to sling some mud your way."

"What?" Kevin cried, rising to his feet.

"Don't get flustered again. I have to consider every possibility. She'd been arguing with her brother. They didn't get on. And you must admit, you'd be an ideal scapegoat for her – if she's been using you."

"She's not!" Kevin exclaimed resentfully.

"Even though you must seem pretty small to her – like David claimed."

"Look . . ." Kevin searched in vain for words strong enough to express his annoyance and deny the detective's charge. "It wasn't her," he retorted. "For one thing, David walked away from her that night."

"He could have gone back."

Kevin shook his head. He would never believe that Ros could either commit a murder or cheat him. "It wasn't her. That's the end of it. She couldn't."

"All right, then. Perhaps, I should put more weight on my other theory."

"What's that?" Kevin snapped.

"That you've staged this whole stunt – in an amazing piece of bravado. A real double bluff. You put the evidence out the back, knowing we'd find it and think it had been planted by someone else. Which is why you've been going round bothering lots of suspects. To make enemies of them."

Kevin was dumbstruck for a few seconds. He

wasn't in the clear, after all. "You . . . you've got a twisted mind," he growled.

"I prefer to call it devious," Charlie replied calmly. "That's why I'm good at my job. Anyway, you and I, we'll have another chat once forensic's finished with the treasure trove in your garden."

When Kevin eventually got rid of the police, he slammed his fist on to the dining table. It hurt quite a lot, but it helped dispel some of his anger.

15

The car plunged suddenly and accelerated alarmingly. Ros's head was thrown back against the cushioned headrest and her stomach seemed to leap, churning her insides. Involuntarily, she let out a scream as the car banked sharply, spiralling down. Despite holding tightly on to the rail, her body was flung sideways, colliding with Kevin. "Aaargh!" she wailed. The wheels clattered and the car jolted first one way, then the other. She slid back across the seat and Kevin slammed into her. A girl in the car behind them screamed at the top of her voice.

The roller coaster braked abruptly. In a series of jolts, it came to a halt. Ros groaned and, still queasy, rose slowly and unsteadily to her feet.

"Okay?" asked Kevin.

"Just about," she answered.

"Told you it was a good ride."

"I'm not sure good is the word I'd use."

"Oh, you loved it really."

"Well . . . I must admit it's a break. Got me out of the house for a bit. But," Ros added, "I still feel guilty about it."

"How about something more leisurely?" Kevin pointed to the lake. "A rowing boat."

"Okay," Ros agreed. "I can show you my rowing skills. Round and round in circles."

They stepped over the narrow-gauge railway line and headed for the wooden jetty.

In an effort to resume a normal life, Ros had decided to ride with Kevin to the leisure park at Billing. Besides, she needed a break after hearing of the find at Kevin's house and Detective Superintendent Whyte's third session with her.

As they glided through the water, scattering the ducks, they talked about the interview. "So," Kevin said to her, "he showed you the torch and asked if you'd seen it before."

"Yes."

"And what did you say?"

"Well, I said that David had one like it. He asked me if David left the house with it that night and I said something along the lines of, 'Now you mention it, I think he did have a torch.' I asked him if he was sure it was David's. He was. Said David's fingerprints were all over it."

"Then, no doubt, he enjoyed telling you where he found it."

"Not exactly. He assumed you'd already told me. He just asked me if there was anything else I'd forgotten to tell him about that night. In an unpleasant sort of way."

"That was my fault. Sorry. I told him you'd mentioned the torch to me. He was grumping because you'd told me but held back the information from him. Anyway," he asked, "you didn't tell him about the photo, did you?"

"No. But I'm no good at this game. I probably blushed."

"Mmm." Kevin looked beyond her and said, "Pull more with the left or we'll end up on dry land."

Ros gave a few strong strokes with her left arm, then said, "If someone planted that stuff on you, who could it have been? Who knows where you live and would want to drop you in it?"

"Well," Kevin replied, "Whyte suggested you."

Ros stopped rowing and exclaimed, "Me!"

"Sorry, but I thought you'd better know," Kevin said. "Of course, I don't . . . Anyway, it's a silly idea. I reckon the list's Chipmonk, Craig Blackstock, or someone at Dearings – maybe Dr Dearing himself or that Frank character."

Ros didn't reply. She was still smarting from the policeman's slur on her character. Absent-mindedly, she resumed rowing.

Kevin changed the subject. "How have you got on? Anything more from the photo or that Channel Islands book?"

"Not really," she replied, trying to forget the accusation. "But there was something in the book about Alderney at the time the photo was taken. Doubt if it's got anything to do with it."

"What?"

"Well, it would have been taken in the early 1940s . . ."

Kevin interrupted, asking, "Wasn't there a war on then?"

"Yes. The Second World War. The Nazis took over the islands. But records of exactly what happened have never been released, according to the book."

"So there was something underhand going on."

"Possibly. No one knows. It may have been some of the islanders co-operating too closely with the enemy. That's what the book suggested. And there was a slave labour camp on Alderney. Many of the prisoners died. I don't know how."

Kevin thought about it for a moment, then said, "You don't think your grandma. . . ?"

"Was a prisoner? I don't know. She could have been, I guess."

"That'd explain why she looked so miserable."

"Yes. It occurred to me, as well. But even if she was, what's it got to do with David?"

"Yeah," Kevin agreed. "And that was fifty years ago. Who's interested in what happened fifty years ago?"

Ros looked at him seriously. "Some are, Kev. Some were hurt so bad they can't forget."

"Look out!" Kevin cried.

It was too late. The prow of the rowing boat parted the reeds at the edge of the lake and ran aground in the mud.

Ros cursed under her breath and Kevin laughed.

He stood up in the boat and said, "Give me one of the oars. I'll get us off."

He positioned the paddle against the bank and pushed hard till the boat floated free of the bottom. Before he sat down again, he glanced at the people on the path who had stopped to watch him wrestling with dry land. For an instant, Kevin caught sight of one particular man just before he turned his face away.

Kevin dropped on to his seat heavily and the boat rocked alarmingly.

"Careful!" Ros chided him. "Come on. Give me the oar."

He handed it over without a comment.

"Are you okay, Kev?" Ros asked.

"Yes. Just get us out of here."

"Why?"

"Because the security guard from Dearings – Frank – is just over there."

"What?" she exclaimed. "Are you sure it's him?"

"Yes. He's behind you. Watching us. Don't turn round. Just get us back."

Ros spun the boat round and headed towards the jetty. "Why?" she said. "Why's he watching us?"

"How should I know?" Kevin replied. "But if he murdered David, and planted the evidence at my place, he could be disappointed that the cops haven't carted me away."

"How do you mean?"

"His ploy didn't work. I haven't been arrested. So he's trying something else to stop me proving he did it."

"You mean he's gunning for you now?" Ros looked petrified. "I told you it was too dangerous, Kev. Ages ago."

"It'll be all right," he assured her. "But we'd better lose him – just in case. And to do that, we need to be on land."

"Okay," she mumbled.

As she rowed back, she thought to herself, "Even if we can lose him here, he knows where Kevin lives."

Back on land, they stood at the edge of the lake and pretended to watch the people playing crazy golf. Ros whispered, "Well? Have you seen him? Is he still watching us?"

"Yes. He's near the entrance to the amusement arcade. Pretending, like us, to be interested in what's going on."

"So how do we lose him?"

"I think we'd better take the train."

"The train?"

"Yes. The trip around the lake."

"But," Ros objected, "he'll just get on one of the carriages."

"Maybe," Kevin replied. "But I don't think so. There are only three small wagons to sit on. He'd have to get too close to us. Blow his cover. My bet is, he'll stay here and watch. The train's in view the whole time and it doesn't stop till we get back here."

"So how are we going to get away from him?" Ros hesitated when she saw the glint in Kevin's eye. "Oh, no!" she murmured. "You're not thinking of jumping off."

Kevin nodded. "I am. Bet it doesn't go that fast. Trust me, it'll be okay."

They got on the train just before it chugged away on its circuit of the lake. As Kevin predicted, the security guard who was tailing them did not attempt to sprint to the train and board it. He stayed at the terminal.

"Okay," Kevin said as the train rattled and

bumped round the track. "We'll jump when we get to the caravan site. We can run among the caravans. It'll be like a maze in there."

"Yes," Ros agreed. "It's in the opposite direction from the car park. If he sees us jump for it, he'll think we're headed away from the bike so he'll run after us. We could double back to the bike and . . . off we go."

"Exactly," Kevin said, impishly.

The wagons lurched round a corner near the caravan park. The train was going no faster than jogging pace. "On your marks," said Kevin. He glanced across the lake and commented, "I can't be sure, but I think he's watching us. It doesn't matter. Get set!" Discreetly, he removed the rope that stretched across the opening. He looked across the lake once more then cried, "Go!"

The train driver turned round and shouted, "Oi! You can't do that!"

But it was too late. In turn, Ros and Kevin had jumped. They were both running as they hit the ground. The other trucks trundled past them and, out of the corner of his eye, Kevin saw the man from Dearing Scientific begin to dash around the perimeter of the lake.

Kevin yelled to Ros, "He's coming after us! But he'll never catch us."

They darted between the closely spaced caravans. Ros swerved to avoid crashing into a dog that was sprawled in their path and, behind her, Kevin jumped over it.

After a burst of sprinting, Kevin called breathlessly, "I'm not as fast as you, remember. And we need to double back."

"Okay," she replied. "Let's turn left down here."

They ran on for a short distance, then turned left again and slowed to jogging pace. Among the forest of caravans, Frank would never find them. Besides, by now he'd be going in the wrong direction.

When they reached the car park, there was no sign of Frank. Quickly, they donned crash helmets and got on the bike. Kevin kick-started it into life, engaged first gear and they rode away at speed.

Before going to his own house, Kevin took Ros home. When she leaned on his good shoulder and swung herself from the bike, she warned him, "Take care, Kev. He knows where you live."

"I know," he replied. "I'll be okay."

"I've been thinking. It could be just that Dr Dearing told him to follow you after you broke in. Maybe that's all it is: checking, in case you try it again or get up to any more funny business."

"That's right. It makes good sense if they still believe their industrial spy theory. Maybe they're tailing me to see who I hand over their industrial secrets to. He might not be after my blood at all." He didn't sound convinced but he smiled at her reassuringly. "By the way," he added, "have you got any stamps?"

"Stamps?"

"As in stamp collecting."

"Yes, I think so. Why?"

"I want them as a bribe to Mr Smith for keeping watch on Dearing Scientific for me," Kevin told her.

"Mother keeps used stamps in a bag. Gives them to charity. I'll see if I can find them for you."

With Ros's bag of stamps in his coat pocket, Kevin rode home via Mr Smith's bungalow.

"Hello, young Kevin," Mr Smith greeted him. "How are you?"

"Okay, thanks," Kevin answered. "Got something for you."

"Oh yes? You'd better come in."

In the lounge, Kevin produced the packet of stamps and the old man's eyes lit up. "Why, thank you!" He took the bag and peered inside.

"Have you got anything for me?" asked Kevin.

"A cup of coffee, perhaps. And a biscuit?" Mr Smith replied.

"No. I mean, anything on Dearings."

"Oh. Are you still into your investigations?"

"'Fraid so."

"Well," Mr Smith said, "I haven't seen anything out of the ordinary. A few more of their vans coming and going, possibly. That's all."

"What sort of vans?"

"Just the usual. All white with that little code on them. Skull and crossbones, with 'Toxic' written underneath."

"Nothing else?"

Mr Smith had been distracted by the contents of the bag of stamps. He was taking them out and examining each one closely as he spoke. "No. Not really."

"How about activities around the school?"

"Er . . . That bully's been up to his usual tricks. Yesterday he pinned one youngster against my wall when the teachers weren't looking."

"How about Chipmonk? Mr Monk, the Deputy Head."

"He's been around, looking sulky. Nothing unusual about that." Mr Smith picked out one of the stamps particularly carefully with tweezers and murmured, "Nice."

Kevin felt he wasn't getting anywhere. He got up to leave. "I'll leave you to get stuck into the stamps – or whatever you do to them."

"Yes. Thank you. Thanks very much," he replied, his head almost inside the bag.

"You'll keep a look-out for me still?"

"Yes. Of course I will."

16

Kevin picked up the spare rib, dripping in barbecue sauce. "Mmm," he said as he tucked in. "That's good." He looked around the American-style café and observed, "It's good in here. Never been able to afford it, though."

Ros, who had agreed to pay the bill, smiled at him. "Wait till you tuck into the chocolate dessert they serve up here."

Kevin glanced at the menu, written on blackboards hung from the ceiling. "'Death by chocolate', they call it," he remarked.

"Yes. Until recently, I liked the name."

"Well, I'll leave some space for it anyway," Kevin replied, gleefully licking the spicy sauce from his fingers.

"Anyway," Ros said seriously, "I only volunteered to bring you here so we could talk something through."

Kevin looked at her and asked, "What's that?"

"Since yesterday at Billing, I've been thinking about this Alderney connection."

"The long-lost-uncle theory?"

"Possibly," Ros answered. "I wonder if we've been barking up the wrong tree."

"Oh?"

"Well, we've been trying to figure out who'd want to kill David." Ros leaned forward and whispered, "But what if David went off to kill someone?"

"How do you mean?"

"If there was a family vendetta of some sort, maybe David set out to end it. He could have brewed up the poison. He was okay at science, you know. But perhaps his intended victim overpowered him and gave David some of his own poison."

Kevin had stopped eating as he listened to her. "So. . . ?" he prompted. Clearly, he wanted to hear more of her line of reasoning.

"So, it could almost have been self-defence. We've been after the murderer. Perhaps we should be looking for an intended victim. That night," she said, "when David walked out, he . . . reacted when I said something about getting his own back.

I was thinking about you, but perhaps he had someone else in mind."

"The missing uncle?"

"Well, it all began on Sports Day, didn't it? Grandfather could have seen his other son," Ros speculated. "He might have whispered it to David. David would have investigated – hence the photo and Channel Islands book. If there really was some bad blood resulting from the Alderney days, David could have confronted him – to settle an old score on behalf of Father or Grandfather. He did love Grandfather, you know."

"Yes," Kevin replied. "But I don't know if you're right. Would your grandad recognize a son after all these years?" He hesitated, then added, "Hang on! Of course he would. Your dad and him were twins. Was there anyone at Sports Day who looked like your dad used to?"

"Not as far as I know. But they may not have been identical twins. Just a bit of family likeness would be enough."

Kevin nibbled at a chip thoughtfully. "He must have changed his name as well. If you're right, at least we know how old this uncle is. You'll even know his birthday. When was it?"

"Boxing Day. Twenty-sixth of December. And he'd be fifty."

"Did you have someone in mind? I think we can rule out Craig Blackstock!"

"I guess so," Ros replied. "There's Edriss, though. And Chipmonk's getting on a bit. I imagine he's about fifty."

"So's Dr Dearing," Kevin put in. "He'd be pretty near perfect – but do you reckon there's a family resemblance?"

"Not really," Ros murmured.

"But there's something I don't understand, if you're right," Kevin said. "How come the fag packets ended up in my garden? If David cooked up the poison, they'd be more likely to turn up in yours."

For a second, Kevin's thoughts turned to Detective Superintendent Whyte's comment, *Ros Rabin might want to sling some mud your way*. If, all along, the family feud had been between Ros and David, maybe she *had* dumped them on him. After all, she had admitted that she felt bitter towards David. Was she so bitter that she was driven to murder? *No*, he told himself. *Don't be ridiculous. It wasn't Ros*. But he couldn't prevent his mind suddenly thinking back to Ros's hobby of macramé. David had been tied to a chair, and Ros was an expert in tying knots in cords that were attached to a chair. She also knew about LD_{50} values.

Ros shrugged. "I don't know how they got there. But nothing's really changed on that score. I'm only suggesting a different motive for the murder. The victim-turned-murderer would still want to put the blame on someone else. It's still got to be someone who knows where you live and that the police are investigating you. Minus Craig Blackstock."

"That rules out Edriss. Unless he's been nosing about without me knowing about it. But we've got nothing on him, just that he smokes and doesn't like kids."

"There is someone else, though."

"Oh?"

"Mr Smith."

"Mr Smith?"

"Yes."

"But," Kevin objected, "he's my mate. And he's nearer his sell-by date than fifty."

Ros shrugged. "He's a nice man, I know, but how much did you tell him? Does he know you're the police's prime suspect?"

"Yes."

"And does he know where you live?"

"I doubt it," Kevin replied.

"In that case, perhaps he's not . . ."

"Just a second," Kevin interrupted. "He does know which road I live in. We chatted about it. So he could've got the house number from the phone book. But . . ." He shook his head. "I can't believe it. If I had a list of people in this world who didn't do it, you'd be number one. He'd be number two."

He wiped his fingers on a serviette and then screwed it up.

They sat in silence while the waiter cleared the table. They resumed their conversation once he'd gone to get the chocolate dessert.

"No," Kevin continued. "He's too old and he doesn't even look like a Rabin."

"That's true," Ros agreed. "But I think he's got to be added to our list."

"You sound like our chum, Whyte. Got to consider every possibility, and all that."

Ros shrugged. "That's true as well."

"Okay," Kevin said, somewhat frostily, "I'll go back tomorrow and ask him when his birthday is. But I bet it's not Boxing Day." Kevin paused before adding, "Hey, that reminds me. Why don't you check out Dr Dearing's birthday? Bet he's in . . . what's that posh people's book called?"

"*Who's Who?*"

"Yeah, that's it. I bet he's in it. And it'll give birthdays, I should think."

"All right, I'll try it. I don't suppose Chipmonk's done enough to get in it as well."

"No," replied Kevin. "That's probably what bugs him."

"Anyway," Ros said, nodding towards the waiter. "Here comes the pudding. Just look at that. Hope you've left enough room."

"Wicked!" Kevin said as the bowl of brown stuff

was slapped down in front of him. "Do you have this often? How come you keep in shape after this?"

"I run it off."

They waded into the dessert.

When they left, neither of them noticed the security officer from Dearing Scientific sitting in a car outside the restaurant. As they strolled along the road towards the shopping centre, the car crawled along behind them at a discreet distance.

17

When he left school the next day, Kevin saw Mr Smith out on his patio, waving to get his attention. Kevin jogged over to the fence and asked excitedly, "Have you seen something?"

"No, not really," he replied. "I just wondered if you could do me a favour."

"Oh?"

"You know those stamps I got the other day? Not yours, the ones that came in the post. Well, I've sorted out what I want and I've got to post the rest back. Would you take the packet to the post office for me? You go past it on the way home, don't you?"

Getting over his disappointment, Kevin answered, "Sure. I'll do that."

"Come round, then. I'll get it for you."

Kevin walked round the garden to the front door. He knocked, then pushed it open and went in. He found Mr Smith in the living room.

"Just sealing it up," the old man said. "Only take a minute."

"You don't collect every single stamp, then?"

"No. That would get out of hand."

"What sort of stuff do you collect? I could keep my eye open for it." Kevin glanced at the table and saw an album open at a page full of old Guernsey stamps. "Guernsey? That's part of the Channel Islands, isn't it?"

"Yes. That's one of the countries I collect."

"I'll see what I can do," Kevin said. "You haven't got a birthday coming up, have you?"

"Birthday?" Mr Smith finished taping up the small parcel and handed it to Kevin.

"Yes," Kevin replied with a smile. "I could put together a packet for your birthday."

The old man returned the smile, genuinely touched by the offer. "No need, lad. Besides, you'd have to wait for next year before I have another birthday. I don't bother with them now. When you get to my age, you forget these things – if you don't have a family to remind you."

Kevin held up the packet and said, "Well, I'll post this for you, anyhow."

"Thanks," he replied. "You're a good lad."

It was only afterwards, as Kevin rode to the post office, that he looked at the address that Mr Smith had scrawled on the package. It was directed to the Channel Islands Stamp Company on Guernsey. Kevin shook his head. He didn't want to make the connection between Mr Smith, the Channel Islands and the Rabins. He hoped it was just co-incidence. Even so, when he got home, he called Ros to tell her about his conversation with Mr Smith.

"Why was he interested in the Channel Islands?" she inquired.

"He might not be. It might be just their stamps. I don't know."

"Didn't you ask?"

"No. Sorry. But he's not your uncle," Kevin argued. "He's ancient. And his birthday's some time early in the year – not December. Unless he was lying, and I don't see why he should be."

"I do," Ros replied. "If he's our man and if he knows we're on to him, of course he'll lie."

"But . . ." Kevin struggled to put into words his objections to her accusation. "Anyone could collect Guernsey stamps. It doesn't mean . . . I just can't believe it's him."

"I know," Ros replied. "And I hope it's not, either. But we've got almost as much evidence against him as anyone else."

"Yes," Kevin admitted unenthusiastically. "You're right. I'd better look into it."

"What will you do? Nothing daft, Kev."

"No," he said into the mouthpiece. "I'll go back tonight and check it out."

"You don't mean break in?"

Kevin had to have the freedom to look around the house without Mr Smith's interference. As the old man hardly ever went out, Kevin would have to give the bungalow the once-over while he slept. He didn't want to worry Ros so he didn't admit it. "No, I'll go and have a chat with him. See what I can find out."

"Be careful, Kev."

"Okay."

"I'll try my luck with Mother again. She's not as doped as she was. I'll see if I can get her to talk about Grandmother and all that."

"Good idea," Kevin answered. "Let me know straightaway if she comes up trumps."

"All right."

"Hopefully, we can clear Mr Smith and then get on to Dearings again. Which reminds me – did you find out Dearing's birthday?"

"Yes," she answered. "Second of May. But there is one thing, Kev."

"Oh yes?"

"His piece in *Who's Who* says he was educated for a while in the Channel Islands."

Kevin perked up. "Really? That's . . . useful to know. I told you – the evidence against him gets stronger all the time. Anything else?"

"No. That's all."

"He's definitely number one, you know. Him, or one of his people."

"You don't think that Dearings man is still following you?"

"I don't think so," Kevin replied. "I think I've shaken him off. Or he's getting better at it."

"Watch out – just in case."

"Every day, Ros, you sound more like a mother!"

Ros giggled nervously. "Sorry. But this is serious stuff. I don't want to lose you, too."

"You won't. I'll be okay. This one's a doddle."

"Yes, I know. But . . . Oh, never mind."

"I'll see you tomorrow," Kevin said. "We'll compare notes then."

"Yes. Sure. 'Bye."

Kevin put down the phone and went to get tea. Then came the eternal wait for nightfall.

Kevin glanced at his watch. Eleven-thirty. He drew the curtain slightly to one side and peered out. Curtis Street was dead. No kids played in the road. Even the men who had spent the evening in the pub had returned to their houses. A few windows glowed by the light within, but most of the terrace was dark. There was not a sound. He scanned the street in both directions, but could see no unfamiliar cars nor any other signs of his watcher. But if Frank was determined to tail him all round the clock, Kevin knew that the guard could be lurking in any one of a hundred shadowy nooks in the street. Kevin let the curtain fall back into place. He sneaked out of the house and closed the front door quietly behind him. He started his bike and accelerated towards School Lane.

He liked the deserted, eerie streets. He could ride fast and cut corners on the wrong side of the road. He even jumped one set of traffic lights.

He stopped and padlocked his bike in the lane beside Mr Edriss's house. Glancing at the living room window, Kevin noted Edriss silhouetted against the light curtain. "It's late for him to be still up," Kevin murmured. "Good job I'm not wanting to do his place tonight – but why should I? I've got nothing on him." Kevin stole past the house and walked towards the bungalow by the school.

18

Ros's mother was sitting up in bed when Ros knocked lightly at the door and stepped inside.

"How are you?" asked Ros.

Her mother shrugged in response.

"Mother," Ros began, "I have to talk to you. I really do. I have to know what happened."

"When?"

"When this photo was taken." Ros showed her David's heirloom. "I need to know if I have an uncle. I need to know what happened to Grandmother. I need to know it all."

"No," her mother replied, refusing to look at the photograph. "Let bygones be bygones. Why can't you let it be?"

"Because it – whatever it is – won't let *me* be."

"What do you mean?"

"I mean, whatever happened to David is getting close to me and Kev."

Her mother looked petrified. "You too? I couldn't bear it if . . ."

"Then you must tell me."

Mrs Rabin didn't reply immediately. She looked everywhere in the room, except at Ros. Then she sighed and said, "It was a long time ago."

"But it's still going on. You have to admit it."

Something inside her mother finally, unwillingly snapped. She nodded tearfully.

"Mother," Ros asked quietly, "do I have an uncle?"

Mrs Rabin covered her face with both hands, shaking her head. "No," her broken voice said.

"But on the back of this photo, it says Grandmother had twins."

"You don't have an uncle." Her mother uncovered her haunted face and whispered, "He died when he was still a baby."

"But . . ." Ros stopped herself. She had a million questions and she didn't know where to start. And her theory about the long-lost uncle was shattered. She sat on the edge of her mother's bed, took her hand and said, "You'd better tell me."

Her mother swallowed. "It's not a nice story," she said. "I don't want you to get hurt as well. But I suppose you have the right to know."

Uncomfortably, she began, "Your grandfather told me something of what happened. It was a bad time for people like him and your grandmother in Alderney."

"When? In the war?"

"Yes. Your grandmother and grandfather were put into a prison – a labour camp on Alderney."

"Why?"

Mrs Rabin shrugged again. "Because they weren't to the soldiers' liking." She squeezed her daughter's hand and continued. "It was a dreadful place, they say. Many died, you know. No one knows quite how many or exactly how they died, but they did. Buried five at a time in unmarked graves, they were. That's where your grandmother and uncle are. Sharing some patch of earth with strangers. At least we know how they died."

"Yes?" Ros prompted sympathetically.

"Most of the islanders hated what was going on during the occupation, but not all. Some helped the soldiers. There was one young man in particular. A new doctor. Doctor Somerton, he was called. He wasn't a bad man, originally. But just before the occupation, he did something both kind and awful. He ended the life of a dying woman. She wanted to die, you understand. She was in great pain. Dr Somerton put an end to her suffering. And his reward? He was struck off. If it hadn't been for the war and the occupation, he'd have

162

been prosecuted. All he had to look forward to after the war was a trial for murder. Under that sort of pressure, he cracked. Maybe he also felt guilty about what he'd done. Maybe it was bitterness about the way he'd been treated. Anyway, he cracked." Mrs Rabin cleared her throat, sniffed and carried on. "They wanted a doctor at the labour camp. He volunteered. The soldiers didn't care that he'd been struck off. All they wanted was someone to make sick people fit for more work and to be experimented on." Her mother wiped her eyes and nose, unable to continue.

Ros waited for a while and then queried, "Experiment?"

"In the war, there were all sorts of atrocities, Ros. The soldiers wanted to know the effects of drugs and chemicals on the human body. Dr Somerton found out. He used the people in the camp as guinea pigs."

"What?" Ros cried.

"They were particularly keen on knowing the effects on pregnant women, apparently. This Dr Somerton fed people with all sorts of pills and potions. Made them breathe all sorts of gases, just to see what happened to them."

"Including Grandmother?" Ros asked in a whisper.

"Yes. She was separated from your grandfather. He was made to work on the island. She was part of the experiment. Dr Somerton did more and more experiments on her and she grew weaker and weaker as her time came. She just had the strength to give birth, but no more. She died afterwards. But," Mrs Rabin sobbed, "that wasn't the end of it. The soldiers and the doctor continued the experiments on the babies."

"No!"

Her mother nodded slowly. "Your father's brother didn't make it. He died after a week, poor little thing! Your father survived, of course, but he was never a well man, as you know. Afterwards, after the war, the hospital tried to find out what he'd been given. They thought he'd been tested with nerve gases, and chemicals from plants like tobacco and deadly nightshade. But they never got to the bottom of it. He'd probably been given all sorts of different things. Ruined his health."

Ros had read about the war. It was part of the curriculum. Yet it had always seemed so distant. It was history. It had happened to someone else, somewhere else. Now, it seemed so close. It involved her family. It had caught up with her as if the whole dreadful business had taken place only yesterday. Its echoes reverberated all about her.

"What happened to Dr Somerton?" she asked.

"No one knows," her mother replied. "After the war, he disappeared. The whole thing was hushed up, but I understand that the authorities did try to find him for a while. They never did, of course. He probably changed his name and . . . just vanished. He got away with it."

"Grandfather tried to find him, too," Ros guessed.

"Yes. And, when he could, so did your father. They searched and searched." She began to sob again. "They wouldn't let it be. Their hate even infected David. They passed it on to him."

"So, after all these years, Grandfather spotted Dr Somerton at Sports Day," Ros surmised. "Could he really have recognized him, fifty years on?"

"You never forget the face of someone who killed your wife and baby. Your grandfather always swore that he'd recognize him any time, any place."

"And he told David who it was."

She nodded. "He must have done. But what's the point, Ros? Whoever he is, he's an old man now. How can you punish him now for what he did then? I don't say he should be forgiven for what he did, but there's nothing that can put matters to right now. He'll have God's judgement soon enough."

"David didn't think like that. He went out to do something about it." Ros was talking to herself really, but she did so aloud.

"Taking the law into your own hands never did any good," her mother replied. "And it won't now."

"But that's what Kev's been doing all along. And," she said, glancing at her watch, "what he might be about to do again right now." She was surprised how long she'd been with her mother, listening to her dreadful story. It was midnight – much later than Ros expected.

"What do you mean?"

"I've got to go and make a call, Mother. But before I do, another question. Do you know who Dr Somerton really is? Did Grandfather or David tell you?"

She shook her head. "No." Her mother called after her, "Don't you get involved as well, Ros. No good can come of it."

Ros hesitated at the door. She looked back at her mother and said, "Just one last thing. Why on earth didn't you tell me all this before?"

Broken, her mother replied, "Because I wanted you to be free of this . . . curse. We tried to protect you."

19

Mr Smith's bungalow was in darkness. The nearby street lamp lit the front porch so Kevin decided to get into the house from the back. Glancing about him to make sure he wasn't being watched, he climbed over the fence and slipped past the garage to the patio at the rear.

Kevin yanked on the patio door in an attempt to slide it back, but it would not budge. It was firmly locked. He crept further along the wall to a window with a fanlight above it. The window itself was not made to open but the fanlight, hinged at the top, was designed to swing outwards. Kevin put his fingers as far as they would go under the lip of the fanlight, and gently pulled outwards. The window didn't move but the wood came away in his hands. It was rotten. He poked at the frame and the end of his finger sank into the crumbling woodwork. "That," he said under his breath, "makes life easier."

From the inner pocket of his jacket, he produced a thin screwdriver and pushed it up under the lip of the wooden frame. It needed only a little force and twisting to go straight through the rotten wood. The tip of the screwdriver emerged on the other side of the window pane, near the catch. Kevin manoeuvred the blade sideways until it was directly under the latch. He thrust it upwards and the bar leapt off its catch.

He put the screwdriver away and pulled open the fanlight. It was only a narrow hole into the house but it was enough. Before he grabbed hold of the decaying frame and heaved himself up and into the bungalow, Kevin hesitated. He didn't doubt his ability to squeeze, head first, through the small opening. He was thinking about what he was doing. Breaking into his friend's home to pry felt like a betrayal. But Ros was right, Mr Smith had become a suspect. He had to be checked out somehow, and Kevin didn't know any other way.

He wriggled through the gap, slowly working his way into the house like a dragonfly struggling to emerge from its larva. With his feet still hooked on the window ledge, Kevin found himself upside down, his outstretched arms reaching down to

Mr Smith's old sofa. He was grateful for the soft landing. He freed his legs and collapsed on to the couch with barely a sound.

He took a small torch from his pocket and flashed the beam about. It was the same old lounge – familiar, unexciting, almost beyond suspicion. What was he looking for? He wasn't entirely sure. Evidence of time spent on Alderney. Evidence of a poison. Anything.

On the table, the torchlight picked out two stamp albums. Kevin flicked the pages. One of the books seemed to contain stamps from Herm, Alderney and Sark and the other from Guernsey and Jersey. Each stamp had a small tag with a number, the year of issue and a brief description. He stopped at a page that bore the title, "1941–44: Issued under British authority during the German Occupation." Kevin groaned and shook his head. "It doesn't mean anything," he reflected. "Doesn't prove he was there. Just that he's interested in the period." He couldn't resist the afterthought, "Like David Rabin."

He flashed the light round the walls and furniture. For the first time, he realized that they were bare of the usual keepsakes – no photographs of a young Mr Smith, of friends or family adorned the room. It was almost as if its occupant didn't have a history – at least not one that could be displayed. That struck Kevin as sad. He wondered what

Mr Smith had done before he retired. The book-shelves revealed an educated man: poetry, plays, natural history and medicine, as well as a variety of stamp catalogues.

In one corner, a few bottles of drink stood on a cabinet with a glass panel. Inside, models of old aeroplanes were displayed. Next to the cabinet, there was an old writing desk and chair. Kevin moved the chair to one side and tried to pull down the front of the bureau but he found that it was locked. Immediately he was curious. There was no key in the lock and the oak front held firm to force. He took from his pocket a length of copper wire and poked it into the lock. After a minute of unsuccessful fishing about in the mechanism, the wire hooked on to the stud. Kevin twisted the wire to imitate the turning of a key. The stud clicked satisfyingly into the unlocked position and the small bolt was withdrawn.

He put the wire away and pulled down the front of the bureau. He sat on the chair as he sifted through the items inside: paper, pens, bills and receipts, a cheque book and a couple of insurance policies. There was a British passport that had never been used and a medical card. Right at the back of the bureau Kevin found a letter, the paper yellow with age. The creases had almost become tears. Obviously, it had been unfolded and read many times over the years. It was from the General

Medical Council, dated June 1940, and was addressed to Dr Somerton of Alderney. The letter informed Dr Somerton that, for purposely ending the life of one of his patients, he had been struck off the medical register and would no longer be permitted to practise medicine.

"Doctor Somerton," Kevin pondered. "Who's he?"

Ros let the phone ring and ring but there was no answer. As usual, Kevin's parents were out till the early hours and obviously Kevin himself wasn't at home. She guessed that he was still at Mr Smith's house. If she wanted to speak to Kevin, she'd have to call Mr Smith.

She put down the phone. While she wondered what to do, she examined the photograph of her grandmother, reduced by Dr Somerton to a physical wreck, and a code number – Rabin 168/EAS. Ros sighed. She had to decide. Was it right to bother an old man by telephoning him at this hour? She guessed that he must be sitting up late with Kevin, so a call wouldn't be too much of an intrusion. She thought that her information was too important to wait till morning, so she really had to talk to Kevin. She was worried about calling, though, because there was a chance that Mr Smith could be Dr Somerton. But if he was, Kevin was in great danger. That would make it even more important to tell Kevin what she knew. She decided to take the risk of telephoning.

First, she had to find Mr Smith's number. In the telephone book, she looked in horror at the sixteen columns of Smiths. Suddenly, it struck her that if someone wanted to disappear by hiding behind a new name, Smith was an excellent choice. A Smith was as safe from discovery as a needle in a haystack.

Ros didn't know the old man's initials, so she ran her finger down the endless list, carefully looking for a Smith that lived in School Lane. It took time but, of all the Smiths, she found only one: Smith, E.A.

Her spine tingled with excitement and fear. It wasn't just the finding of his name and number that thrilled and scared her. There was something else.

"Mr E.A. Smith," she said to herself. She looked again at the back of her grandmother's photograph and read, "Rabin 168/EAS. I wonder if they're initials. EAS. Does it stand for Dr E.A. Somerton? And now Mr E.A. Smith!" It was too close a match to be coincidence. "It's him!" she said to herself. "He just changed Somerton to Smith."

Her hair seemed to stand on end. It was like the sensation before a big race – the excitement, the nerves. But now the stakes were much higher. Ros knew that a phone call wasn't enough any more.

Kevin was in trouble. Real trouble. She grabbed a coat and dashed out of the house. She had no idea what she had to do. There was no plan in her head. She knew only that she had to get to Mr Smith's house. She was running the most important race of her life.

Kevin was so engrossed in reading the letter that he didn't hear Mr Smith coming up behind him. He nearly leapt out of the chair when the gun was placed against the back of his neck.

"Don't move!" the old man ordered. "Put your hands behind the chair."

Kevin didn't dare speak. He simply obeyed.

"I'm going to put the gun down and tie you up. Don't think I can't pick it up if you make a move."

Kevin let out a yelp as the cord from Mr Smith's dressing gown was tightened roughly around his wrists, anchoring them to the framework of the chair.

"Right," said the old man, retreating towards the doorway and the light switch. "Let's see what I've caught."

When the room filled with light, both of them blinked but Mr Smith was the first to react. "Kevin!" he cried in surprise.

Kevin looked at his friend but said nothing. He didn't know what to say.

"So," Mr Smith said, as he recovered from the

initial shock, "you've figured it out. You know." The old man put the revolver away in the pocket of his dressing gown. "I did wonder – when you got inquisitive."

Behind his back, Kevin tried to loosen the knot by twisting his wrists, but there was no play in the cord. Mr Smith had secured him well. There was no chance of escaping from the chair.

His captor sighed heavily and approached the writing desk. He took the letter and waved it in front of Kevin before replacing it in the bureau. "You've read this, as well," he murmured. "I wish you hadn't. And I wish it wasn't you. But you leave me no choice."

Reaching into a cupboard, Mr Smith produced a bottle of rum. He unscrewed the top and smelled the liquid. He turned up his nose and said, "This is a little something Rabin made for me. It's your turn now."

20

With his arms bent round the chair, Kevin's shoulders were forced backwards. A dull ache had set in, especially in the left shoulder that had been injured by the spike. The back of the chair dug into the tops of his arms and his muscles blazed with pain. Tied tightly at the wrists, one hand had become numb. Pins and needles jabbed at the other.

"It's my own fault," Mr Smith mumbled, partly to himself, partly to Kevin. "I destroyed every trace of my former life. Everything except that letter. I should have got rid of that as well. But I couldn't bring myself to burn it. I needed it to remind me of what they did to me. They destroyed my career before it had hardly begun. *They* started this whole thing."

"You were Dr Somerton?" asked Kevin.

Clutching the bottle of rum to his chest as if it were a new-born baby, Mr Smith glanced at Kevin. "You don't know everything, then."

"I don't know anything."

The old man sniggered. "Don't try and wangle your way out of this by pretending to be ignorant. It's too late for that. You wouldn't be here if you weren't on to me." He ambled restlessly round the room as he spoke. "Why did you come here in the first place?"

Kevin nodded towards the table. "The stamps."

"Stamps?"

"It connected you with the Channel Islands and Alderney."

"Is that all?"

"No. You knew where I lived. You could've planted the torch and fag packets on me. But," Kevin reasoned, "it doesn't matter now. I'm here. Plenty of people know I'm here. They'll come for me. You can't get away with it. You might as well let me go."

"You're wrong," Mr Smith replied, approaching him. "I *can* get away with it. The police don't suspect me. They suspect you. You told me. They think you made this." He held up the bottle. "When they find you, it will all make sense. You were filled with remorse and the police were closing in on you. You took your own medicine." He brought the bottle to Kevin's lips and tilted it. Kevin kept his mouth shut, but the old man grabbed him by his hair and yanked his head back. Kevin let out a cry and at that moment his mouth filled with the vile liquid.

"Ugh!" He spat out most of the rum on to the carpet but couldn't help swallowing some of the poison. It left an acrid, burning sensation in his mouth and his stomach churned.

"I had the boy Rabin tied up in this same chair," Mr Smith said, standing back and examining his prisoner. "Found him here in the dead of night. He'd obviously found out who I am. After all these years. The Rabins hadn't forgotten. They'd stumbled on me here. The boy thought he could get his own back, putting something in my rum. But I surprised him. Tied him up, and turned the tables on him. I fed him his own cocktail. Just a little at a time," Mr Smith said menacingly. "A lot at once and it would just come up again. That'd do no good."

The old man jammed the bottle into Kevin's mouth again, ramming it painfully against his teeth. Kevin swallowed a little more. His mouth and throat felt foul.

This time, as his head went back, his eyes were open and he spotted something – a face at the window. He couldn't see who it was – the face appeared dimly for an instant, then it was gone.

But Mr Smith had his back to it. If someone had come to rescue Kevin, the old man was fortunately unaware of it. Kevin prayed that the person at the window would come in quickly, before he was forced to drink any more. He tried to keep Mr Smith talking, knowing that if the old man was speaking there would be less time for poisoning.

"Why did you kill David Rabin?"

"I had no quarrel with him, it's true. But he was trying to kill me. He failed. If he'd lived, he would have turned me in. I'll not be exposed by the Rabin family or by anyone else." He stared at Kevin for a moment, then added, "I won't be tried as some inhuman war criminal. I won't be humiliated. I'll do anything to avoid that. Anything!"

"How come you got hold of those fag packets and put them in my garden?"

"Ah, yes. When he came here – Rabin – he had a plastic bag full of cigarette packets. It didn't take much imagination to work out what he'd put in the rum. Nicotine! And he'd brought the packets, so his plan was to force me to drink it and then leave the packets here to make it look as if I'd killed myself," Mr Smith ranted. "Suicide! He'd have revealed my past, no doubt, to make suicide seem credible. Well, I gave him a good dose of the rum he'd doctored and threw him out. I kept his torch and the packets. I knew that old Edriss up the road has a reputation for hating kids –

everyone knows it – so I left the evidence in his garden. I thought the police would check him over as an obvious suspect and find them. Only a matter of time before the clues were found. But, then, one night you came along. Pity it was you," Mr Smith muttered. "Anyway, you volunteered the information that the police were on to you. Ideal! I went back to Edriss's garden that night – the silly fool nearly caught me, actually – and got them back."

"Then you planted them at my place," Kevin deduced.

"Yes." Mr Smith smiled. It was no longer the smile of a harmless pensioner, but that of a scheming madman. He approached Kevin again. "Time for more!"

"No!"

But the neck of the bottle was in his mouth and the evil drink hit his throat like acid. Spluttering and coughing, some of the liquid trickled from his mouth, down his chin and on to his shirt. Kevin felt his body twitching. He couldn't control it. He was on the point of vomiting but he couldn't quite bring up the fluid. His eyes flickered and his head ached. He felt dizzy with the alcohol that had been forced into him. Just as he was beginning to think he must have imagined the face at the window, there was a loud thump at the front door as someone barged into it, smashing a way into the house. Kevin sighed with relief. His rescuer! "Quickly!" he urged.

Mr Smith stumbled across the room and hid behind the living room door. The gun was in his hand again.

The door swung open slowly then, suddenly, someone stepped into the room.

Kevin cried, "Watch out!"

It was too late. Mr Smith slammed the butt of the gun down on the back of the intruder's head and the figure slumped on to the floor.

The old man turned the body over with his foot so it lay on its back, staring at the ceiling. "Who's this?" he asked Kevin.

Kevin stared across the room. For a moment, he didn't recognize the body lying on the rug. He thought it might have been Ros coming to his rescue. After all, she knew where he was. But it wasn't Ros. It was Dearings' security guard who lay, stunned, on the floor. Even though Kevin hadn't noticed him earlier, he must have followed him to Mr Smith's home. "Frank," Kevin replied. "He's from Dearing Scientific. I thought he was the murderer." At least, Kevin thought to himself, it wasn't Ros who had been slugged. He wanted to escape, he wanted her help – but he didn't want her to get hurt as well.

Mr Smith surveyed the body littering his living room. "Mmm. How very convenient."

"What?" Kevin whimpered.

Mr Smith left the room briefly. When he returned, he was carrying a syringe.

"What are you doing?" Kevin asked in a slurred voice.

"I'm glad I kept David Rabin's concoction," he replied, "but there's not much left." He tipped a little of the deadly rum into a glass and filled the barrel of the syringe from the tumbler. "It's far more potent by intravenous injection. My own experiments years ago confirmed that." He held up the syringe and examined it. "I need enough for you to drink so this fellow will have to have it by injection."

"No!" Kevin cried. "Why? He's done you no harm."

"He's seen you and me. And," Mr Smith added, "he's your second victim."

Kevin was confused. He couldn't figure it out. "How do you mean?" he asked.

"You're the murderer and you've been pestering Dearings. In response, one of them started to pester you. So, to get him off your back, you kill him. I'll make sure your fingerprints are on this," Mr Smith indicated the syringe filled with brown liquid, "before dumping his body on the field. It's the second murder that makes you finally snap. That's when you decide to kill yourself with the poison. You'll be found on the field as well."

Kevin couldn't concentrate on words. He could take in one sentence but missed the next altogether. Even so, he understood enough of what Mr Smith was plotting.

The old man was warped, consumed with malice over a fifty-year-old decision to end his career. He wasn't Ros's uncle but in some way he'd tangled with the Rabins on Alderney. David had planned to finish the whole rotten business by killing him. Yet David's attempt had backfired. Now, the feud between Dr Somerton and the Rabins was as keen and alive today as it was all that time ago. They all felt aggrieved by past events. They had all been tormented too much to forgive and forget.

Kevin couldn't focus properly but he saw Mr Smith kneeling where Frank was laid on the floor and then rising. He seemed to be wiping the syringe with a handkerchief. Next, Kevin felt Mr Smith behind him, pressing the syringe into his palm and closing his numb fingers around it.

The old man reappeared in front of him, clutching the bottle in one hand. He peered closely into Kevin's eyes and said, "You won't need much more."

The rum ran into his mouth again. Kevin was beyond struggling. He had no resistance. He gulped down the whole mouthful and immediately retched. He was not sick enough, though. Most of the nicotine stayed in his body. As he neared the lethal dose, the poison sapped his strength and robbed him of his control and capacity to reason. His head lolled helplessly to one side.

Breathless, Ros arrived at Mr Smith's front door. She was surprised to find it ajar. She peered into a darkened hall. She was tempted to call out to Kevin but, fearing that he was with Mr Smith, she did not want to forewarn the man who had once been Kevin's friend. She pushed the door open and stepped quietly into the hall. She didn't know where they were, so she had to try each room in turn. Noiselessly and nervously, she opened the door of the first room on the left. It was dark inside. Even so, she realized that it was a bathroom. She left straight away. On the other side of the hall, she tried another door but found herself in another unlit room. This time, it was a bedroom.

She turned into the main corridor. At the far end, it led into the kitchen where a striplight shone brightly. She could not hear voices, though, so guessed that Kevin and Mr Smith were in one of the two rooms between her and the kitchen.

Slowly and carefully, she turned the knob on the first door and opened it a crack. A band of light appeared. The room was lit and muttering issued from the other side of the door. Her heart raced. This was it. She took a deep breath and walked into the lounge.

Kevin was writhing horribly in a chair and Mr Smith was standing over him like a vulture. Realizing that someone had entered the room, the old man spun round, his hand darting to his dressing-gown pocket.

Ros saw the gun in Mr Smith's hand. She tried to dash for cover but she tripped over a body on the floor and landed in a heap.

The gun exploded. The bullet, missing Ros, thudded into Frank's body. Ros screamed.

"You're David Rabin's sister," the old man barked. An insane grin came to his face as he aimed the gun at her again.

Ros winced. She wanted to cover her head with her hands and cower on the floor but some inner strength prevented terror taking over. She fixed her eyes on him and said, "Why are you hesitating, Dr Somerton? Why not shoot? You killed most of the rest of my family. Why not me as well?" She crouched on the floor defiantly and answered her own question. "You were good once. You cared. Cared too much, maybe. You got punished for it. You got your own back by punishing those poor people on Alderney. You used up all your hatred on people like my grandmother. You haven't got enough left after all this time to kill me as well." Sweat gathered on her brow. The gun was still pointed at her but it hadn't been fired. At least Mr Smith was listening to her so she carried on talking. "I haven't come for revenge like David. I'm not here to judge you. I only came for Kevin. I'll walk out of here with him. That's all I want." She clung to the sofa and, shakily, pulled herself to her feet. "Let me take him."

"No." Mr Smith still held the bottle of rum in one hand. With the other, he thrust the gun directly towards Ros and began to squeeze the trigger. "You're lying. You're Rabin's sister. You're like him. But I won't let you drag me through the dirt."

"No," she said in a quaking voice. "It all happened years before I was born. I've got no right to sit in judgement. And I know you didn't start it. I can't condemn you – or forgive you. But I'm not going to let you finish it by killing Kevin."

"I don't need your pity, young lady. And, as for him," Mr Smith gestured towards the sad figure tied to the chair, "he's already had a lethal dose. It's too late."

"What?" Ros shrieked.

"It doesn't finish with him," he said to Ros. "It finishes with you." His forefinger pulled the trigger. He was so close to her, he couldn't miss.

Behind him, Kevin jerked upright. He was too confused to work out what was happening but, with Mr Smith distracted, he saw an opportunity. He lifted his right leg and rammed it into Mr Smith's thigh.

The old man twisted and crumpled. The gun went off. The shot hit Ros's shoulder and then slammed into a wall-clock. The clock chimed ridiculously twice, then fell silent. The bottle slipped from Mr Smith's grasp and rolled towards Ros. As it moved, the remaining liquid spilled on to the carpet, leaving a brown trail across the floor like a bloodstain.

Mr Smith's head appeared over the sofa and he prepared to fire again at Ros. Ros bent down, hardly noticing the pain in her shoulder, picked up the bottle and hurled it at the old man.

With a sickening thud, the glass caught him directly on the forehead. The gun flew out of his hand. His eyes stared in surprise and some rum ran down his cheek. He collapsed, unconscious.

Ros rushed to Kevin. As soon as she untied the cord that held him to the chair, he keeled over. Ignoring the agony of her wound, she helped him to his feet and shouted, "Kev! Kev!"

He groaned, barely aware of her.

"Don't let me down now," she bellowed at him. "Come to!"

Kevin croaked, "Ugh! Got to be sick."

"What? How?"

"Got to get it out of my system," he spluttered.

Ros glanced around the room as if looking for something to make Kevin vomit. There was nothing. "Oh, well," she said, steeling herself, "here goes." She held him up with her left arm and swung her right as hard as she could, landing a heavy punch in his stomach.

Kevin uttered a deep inhuman moan, "Ugh!" He slipped from her grasp, dropped to his knees and was immediately sick.

Ros knelt down, fearing that she had finished him off herself. Clutching his heaving shoulders, she lamented, "What have I done?"

Kevin, his face completely drained of colour, twisted towards her and gurgled, "You might have saved my life." He looked away, wailed involuntarily and was sick again.

When he'd finished, Ros yanked him to his feet. "Can you walk?"

"No," he replied.

Ros glanced at Mr Smith, who was beginning to stir. "Tough," she said. "You'll have to." Then she added, "Just a second." She kicked Mr Smith's gun under a sideboard where it was out of sight. "Don't want him shooting at us down the street."

Supporting Kevin as best she could, she guided him out of the room. She steered him as rapidly as possible through the hall and out into the blissfully quiet night.

"There," she said, pointing to a telephone box about a hundred metres up the road. "We'll call for help from there. Can you make it?"

"I don't know."

Together they staggered along the pavement, away from Mr Smith's bungalow. Kevin stopped to vomit painfully yet again. "Good," Ros encouraged him. "The more that comes up, the better."

Eventually they made it. Propping him up in the telephone box, she called for an ambulance.

Ros didn't have to call the police. Neighbours, awakened by the gunshots, had already alerted them. But when they arrived at the bungalow, there was no one to arrest.

Mr Smith had emptied the dregs of the bottle of rum into his own veins. The syringe lay a few centimetres from his frozen, outstreched hand. He had injected the poison directly into his blood-stream. It had killed him rapidly and efficiently.

He had turned the smoking gun on himself.

21

Ros looked through the window into the corridor. There were some people milling about, but the way seemed clear. She slipped through the door and padded along to Room 216. She gripped the handle, looked about to make sure that no one was watching her, opened the door cautiously and edged inside.

"Hi!" Kevin said brightly from the bed.

"Sssh!" Ros closed the door before speaking. "They told me I couldn't see you. I shouldn't be here."

"Why not?"

"You need to sleep it off. You need rest, they said."

"Well, they let Detective Superintendent Whyte in, a while back."

"That's because *he's* important. He saw me too, by the way."

"To take a statement?" asked Kevin.

"Yes."

"How's the shoulder? The sling looks impressive. Do you really need it or is it a new fashion thing?"

Ros laughed. "No. The bullet made more of a mess than I thought at the time. When I injure a shoulder, I'm not like you – I make a real job of it. They've plastered it so it keeps still while it heals. How about you, though? How do you feel?" Ros sat on the hospital bed to hear his reply.

"I'm okay," Kevin answered. "My arms feel like they've been in a straight-jacket for a year. My head feels like a huge boulder that's about to roll off my shoulders. My stomach . . . Well, it feels like I've had two curries from the salmonella van outside the club."

"Oh well," Ros replied cheekily, "no problem, then." She glanced round and asked, "How come you got a room to yourself? I didn't."

"It's not for my benefit. It seems that the other patients wouldn't have enjoyed seeing, hearing and smelling the effects of the treatment I had to have."

"Ugh! Don't tell me any more." Changing the subject, she asked, "Did Detective Superintendent Whyte tell you about Frank?"

"Yeah. He didn't make it," he answered

gloomily. "Pity, because he must have seen through the window that I was in trouble and came in to help me. Whyte found out that we were right about him, by the way. He was following me because, after I broke in, Dearing ordered him to. Thought I was some sort of industrial spy or troublemaker. Must be paranoid about security. He wanted to know who I talked to, in case I was passing all his secrets to an environmental pressure group, a rival, or to the press. Anyway, Frank would have survived the shooting, Whyte said, but the poison got him."

"And Mr Smith? Or should I say Dr Somerton?"

Kevin nodded. "I should hate him, I suppose, after what he did to me but . . . I don't know . . . I just feel sad for him. He'd flipped his lid, obviously, but even so . . ."

"I know what you mean," Ros replied. "It was something that should have been left behind fifty years ago. But it all happened yesterday. Think of it as something left over from the war. That way, it belongs to history. Makes it more remote. It's easier that way."

"I guess so."

Standing up, Ros commented, "I'd better go. Before I get caught." She pointed to the anti-smoking poster on the wall opposite Kevin's bed and said, "Promise me you won't ever take up smoking again."

Kevin smiled. "I don't want to see another ciggie for as long as I live."

"Good."

"Before you go," Kevin called after her, "promise me you won't ever take up a career in boxing." He rubbed his tender midriff.

"Don't worry," Ros replied. "I haven't got the stomach for it, either."

If only he had felt fit enough, he'd have thrown one of his pillows at her. Instead, he groaned and pulled the sheet up over his head.

Malcom Rose

While studying for a degree in chemistry at York University, Malcolm began to write fiction as a hobby – a release from the rigorous confines of science. Now, as a lecturer in Chemistry at The Open University, he combines his enthusiasm for writing with his scientific background by producing texts for distance teaching. His interest in fiction is as strong as ever and he has published three novels in the Adlib series for Scholastic Children's Books. As a novelist, he likes to tackle contemporary issues in tense thrillers, sometimes with a scientific theme.

Malcom is also the author of a chemistry text-book and many scientific papers, and has edited a chemistry periodical. His current research includes chemical aspects of sudden infant death. Born in Coventry in 1953, he now lives with his wife and son in Milton Keynes.

Coming soon in the Point Crime series . . .

Baa Baa Dead Sheep
Jill Bennett

The theatre was in darkness still. Light flooded the scene dock as Beth touched the switch and went to drop her basket in its usual spot by the prop gallery steps. She listened but everything was quiet. Shrugging her shoulders she pulled out a sheet of paper and attached it to the scene dock wall with sticky tape. It was a list of things to be done for the gang of SAPS who had volunteered to build and paint the rather elaborate scenery for *Bella*. They were due in any time after ten o'clock.

Beth looked around, there was nothing out of place. Burglars? Well, they'd be gone by now and what was done was done.

She armed herself with three reels of different coloured masking tape and set off for the stage. Each act of the play had to have its furniture and entrances marked out on the floor of the stage with a different coloured tape. This helped the stage staff to know exactly where to put the furniture and also helped the actors to learn their moves more precisely.

Beth went through the passage to the green room switching on the lights. Nothing was out of place but there was a rather marked smell as she passed through it.

Some perfume, she thought, to hang about all night! Perhaps its the new stuff Jo's using for cleaning make-up off collars.

Gathering speed, she ran up the last steps onto the stage two at a time. The switch for the two great working spots was on a brick pillar just below the lighting gallery. It always made a most satisfying click when it was turned on or off. It did so today.

Light, white and harsh, flooded the area.

Nothing prepared Beth for what she saw.

Her feet were standing in a pool of red.

Within an inch of her shoe, also lying in the red pool, was the body of a man.

He lay completely still with both arms outstretched and his head turned away from her.

He seemed to be red all over. Then Beth saw the bucket. That too was lying on its side. It was the boys' blood bucket – now quite empty.

George Lamb. Baa-Baa. Caretaker, was dead as mutton.

P●INT CRiME

If you like Point Horror, you'll love Point Crime!

A murder has been committed . . . Whodunnit?
Was it the teacher, the schoolgirl, or the best friend? An exciting new series of crime novels, with tortuous plots and lots of suspects, designed to keep the reader guessing till the very last page.

School for Death
Peter Beere
When the French teacher is found, drowned in the pond, Ali and her friends are plunged into a frightening nightmare. Murder has come to Summervale School, and *anyone* could be the next victim . . .

Shoot the Teacher
David Belbin
Adam Lane, new to Beechwood Grange, finds himself thrust into the middle of a murder investigation, when the headteacher is found shot dead. And the shootings have only just begun . . .

Look out for:

Baa Baa Dead Sheep
Jill Bennett
Mr Lamb, resident caretaker of the *Tree Theatre*, has been murdered, and more than one person at the theatre had cause to hate him . . .

Avenging Angel
David Belbin
When Angelo Coppola is killed in a hit-and-run accident, his sister, Clare, sets out to find his killer . . .

POINT HORROR
Read if you dare. . . .

Are you hooked on horror? Are you thrilled by fear? Then these are the books for you. A powerful series of horror fiction designed to keep you quaking in your shoes.

Also in the Point Horror series:

Beach House
The Hitchhiker
by R.L. Stine

The Cheerleader
The Return of the Vampire
The Perfume
by Caroline B. Cooney

The Waitress
by Sinclair Smith

The Cemetery
by D.E. Athkins

Point Romance

If you like Point Horror, you'll love Point Romance!

Anyone can hear the language of love.

Are you burning with passion, and aching with desire? Then these are the books for you! Point Romance brings you passion, romance, heartache, and most of all, *love* . . .

Saturday Night
Caroline B. Cooney

Summer Dreams, Winter Love
Mary Francis Shura

The Last Great Summer
Carol Stanley

Last Dance
Caroline B. Cooney

Cradle Snatcher
Alison Creaghan

Look out for:

New Year's Eve
Caroline B. Cooney

Kiss Me Stupid
Alison Creaghan

Summer Nights
Caroline B. Cooney

THE UNDERWORLD TRILOGY
Peter Beere

When life became impossible for the homeless of London many left the streets to live beneath the earth. They made their homes in the corridors and caves of the Underground. They gave their home a name. They called it UNDERWORLD.

UNDERWORLD
It was hard for Sarah to remember how long she'd been down there, but it sometimes seemed like forever. It was hard to remember a life on the outside. It was hard to remember the real world. Now it seemed that there was nothing but creeping on through the darkness, there was nothing but whispering and secrecy.

And in the darkness lay a man who was waiting to kill her . . .

UNDERWORLD II
"Tracey," she called quietly. No one answered. There was only the dark threatening void which forms Underworld. It's a place people can get lost in, people can disappear in. It's not a place for young girls whose big sisters have deserted them. Mandy didn't know what to do. She didn't know what had swept her sister and her friends from Underworld. All she knew was that Tracey had gone off and left her on her own.

UNDERWORLD III
Whose idea was it? Emma didn't know and now it didn't matter anyway. It was probably Adam who had said, "Let's go down and look round the Underground." It was something to tell their friends about, something new to try. To boast that they had been inside the secret Underworld, a place no one talked about, but everyone knew was there.

It had all seemed like a great adventure, until they found the gun . . .